THE FACE OF ABRAHAM CANDLE

BY BRUCE CLEMENTS

Two Against the Tide

The Face of Abraham Candle

THE FACE OF ABRAHAM CANDLE

by Bruce Clements

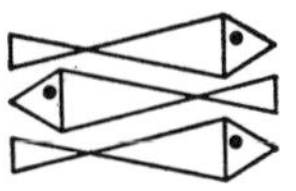

FARRAR, STRAUS & GIROUX
New York
A BELL BOOK

First printing, 1969
Library of Congress catalog card number: 74–85365

Printed in the United States of America
Published simultaneously in Canada by
Doubleday Canada, Ltd., Toronto
Designed by Betty Crumley

For two friends, Bill and Louise

I thank Mr. Elvin T. Cobb and Mrs. Helen Daniels of Durango, Colorado; the Reverend Mr. Homer Root and Mrs. Marguerita Norton of Fort Lewis College, Durango; Mrs. Jerry McCabe of the Mancos, Colorado, Library; Mr. and Mrs. William Little of La Plata Canyon, Colorado; Ellen Holsten of Mancos, and Mr. and Mrs. Samuel Avis of Silverton, Colorado; Mr. Gilbert Wenger, chief archaeologist at the Mesa Verde National Park, and Mr. Jack Rudy of the National Park Service, Washington, D.C., for helping me get ready to write this novel.

Part I

1

Abraham Candle and Jane Stent sat looking at each other on Abraham's bed.

"I'm going to the Placer Hole tonight and play blackjack," he said, reaching into his pocket. "You know blackjack? It's a card game. Here." He took Jane's hand and dropped four gold coins into it. "Pretty, aren't they? They're called Quarter Eagles. There are four of them."

"Four," Jane said.

"Altogether they're worth ten dollars. And if I lose, it's all right. I can afford it."

He took the coins out of her hand. She looked unhappy. "Maybe I'll win," he said. "If I win, I'll buy you a present. What would you like?"

Jane stood up on the hard, narrow bed, turned

around and walked to the end of it, leaving a big wet spot on the blanket. Abraham got up, grabbed her, and put her on the floor. She started to cry. "I don't like to sleep on a wet bed," he said. "Come on, let's play some cards. I'll teach you how to play blackjack. If you know how to play blackjack, you can face the world, even if you're only two."

Abraham went and took his deck of cards off the bureau. As he picked it up, he glanced at his face in the mirror. It wasn't a bad-looking face. It was open, honest, and even intelligent. But it was a young face, younger than he wanted it to be. And it never seemed to get older. That's why he wanted to go away, not just to get out of this house, or find something exciting to do, or make money, but to give his face a chance to change. Maybe, if he went away, it would change for the better. Maybe it would get to look more like his father's face.

He sat back down and dealt two pair. "Mr. Candle and I used to play cards every Saturday night. Do you remember him? He used to carry you around and play with you and tell you long stories. You liked him."

"Alone," she said.

Abraham shook his head. "No, not Mr. Malone, Mr. Malone is somebody else. I'm talking about Mr. Candle. He was bigger than Mr. Malone. He used to walk back and forth with you and tell you stories when you were very small. I guess you don't remember him."

He looked at her cards. The king of diamonds was up. "Now here's the way you play the game," he said, "You want to get twenty-one points, or close to it, without going over."

She picked up her cards and put them in her mouth.

"Don't eat those things," he said. "They're dirty."

"I'm home, Abraham."

It was Mrs. Stent, standing in the doorway behind him. She was a tall, sloppy woman with long hair twisted into a bun at the back of her head. Every Sunday morning she undid it and brushed it and put it up again, but it always looked the same. A lot of it got into the food she cooked. It was brown and very fine, like spiderweb threads.

Abraham stood up. So did Jane. "Good evening, Mrs. Stent," he said.

"Are Julie and Robie anywhere?" she asked. She had a soft voice, sweet and far away and a little bit foolish.

"The last time I saw them, they were in the back yard," Abraham said.

"Play cards!" Jane said.

Abraham looked at her. She had a beautiful face. "We'll play blackjack later."

Mrs. Stent gave a little shrug. "They're not there now. I just came in that way."

"I'll get them," Abraham said. "I told them not to go any place after dinner."

He took the cards from Jane and put them in his pocket, went through the kitchen, out the back door, across the back yard, over the fence, and started up the rocky hill behind the house. He liked going after the children because it gave him a chance to climb, and that's what he was good at. He was fast, he was careful, he could think ahead, and he had good balance.

"Abraham," his father said to him once, "you're a climber. If you couldn't find a hill to climb up, you'd find a hole to climb down. And if there were no hills, and no holes, you'd start at your toes and climb yourself."

At the top of the hill there was a level place with some large spruce trees on it. Beyond the trees stood Anvil Mountain, a high, desolate hump of rock reaching up toward the sky. Where the mountain began there was a cave, hidden by some boulders, where Julie and Robie sometimes went to play and hide. To please them, Abraham pretended not to know where it was.

He got to the trees and stopped. "Robie! Julie!" he shouted. Then he turned around, sat down on a rock, and looked down at Silverton. A pack train was going along Iron Street toward the railroad station. He counted the burros, seventeen, loaded down with bags of silver ore on their way to the smelter in Durango.

"I'll go some place else," Abraham said to himself. "It's time. Inside a week, maybe tomorrow or the next day, I'll be gone. Maybe Kansas. Or maybe I'll go to sea."

He heard Julie and Robie yelling. They were racing from the cave to see which one could get to him first. Instead of waiting for them, as he usually did, he started quickly down the slope toward the house.

Julie Stent was nine and Robie Stent was seven. Abraham told them stories at night. The hero of his stories was "The Great McGregor, the Lone Hero of Colorado." The Great McGregor was unbelievable. He kept gold and silver mines from falling into the hands of evil English bankers. He rescued freezing, starving children trapped in abandoned cabins high up on the sides of steep mountains. He caught flying bullets with his bare hands. He started snowslides rushing down mountains, crushing schoolhouses and sweeping away mean teachers, but leaving the children inside untouched. The Great McGregor, at all times and in all places, did things that only the Great McGregor could do.

Half an hour after Abraham had called them, Julie

and Robie were in their nightshirts at the kitchen table drinking oat milk, which Mrs. Stent made by adding almond extract and sugar to the water of boiled oats, and waiting to hear the next chapter of "The Great McGregor and the River Beneath the Mountain." Mrs. Stent was leaning against the stove with a piece of wood in her hand, waiting too. Jane was in her crib in the front room, asleep.

"Well," Abraham said, "you remember how in the last chapter of 'The Great McGregor and the River Beneath the Mountain' the Great McGregor, after a long, hard climb up the cliff, was just about to go into the Black Cave where the Black Octopus was coming after Elizabeth and Freemont."

Abraham stopped for a moment to figure out what should happen next. He knew that sooner or later the Great McGregor, alone and without help of any kind, would defeat the Black Octopus, swim the river, and save the children. And he knew that because of their adventure Elizabeth and Freemont would learn some great lesson about life and become better children. But that was all he knew.

"What'd he do?" Robie asked.

"Well," Abraham said, "he was just about to go into the cave when he thought of something very important that he hadn't thought of before. He thought of being thirsty. He remembered that he was thirsty. That was the one thing about the Great McGregor that nobody knew, that when he got thirsty he had to have a drink before he could do anything else. He suddenly felt thirstier than he had ever felt in his life. So he looked around to see if there was a spring anywhere. And he looked and he looked and he looked, but he couldn't see one. Just then he heard the sound of water up the mountain beyond the cliff. He wondered what he should do, if he should go down into the cave, or if he should climb up and look for the water."

Abraham stopped. Julie and Robie watched him, troubled. Mrs. Stent pulled a piece of bark from the stick in her hand and threw it into the stove. "Then what?" Julie said, and Abraham started again. He told how the Great McGregor searched for the hidden stream of water, climbing higher and higher up the steep mountain. He told how the sound of water led the lone hero farther and farther on, getting thirstier and thirstier. Finally he told how the Great McGregor reached the top of the mountain and found a spring bubbling out of a rock. "It was beautiful water," Abraham said, "and especially beautiful because the Great McGregor was so thirsty. So he kneeled down, and he was just about to drink, when a voice behind him said, 'Don't drink. If you drink, you die.'

"And I'll tell you what happened after that tomorrow night. Now your mother wants you to go to bed."

The children begged him to go on, but he said no, partly because he wanted to get to the Placer Hole, and partly because he didn't know what was going to happen next. "I'll give you a hint, though," he said. "The person who told him not to drink was a woman."

Robie twisted up his face. "A woman, on top of a mountain?"

"Women can climb mountains," Abraham said. He stood up. "I'm going out for a while, Mrs. Stent."

"Will you be back soon?" she asked.

"I won't be too late," he said, "but I don't want to keep you up waiting for me."

"Where are you going?"

"To the Placer Hole."

"What are you going to do in a place like that?"

"Gamble."

He bent over and kissed Robie on the forehead, said good night to Julie, went out through the kitchen door, walked around to the front of the house, crossed the road, cut through the corral of Calkin's Horse and Burro Stable, and started toward Blair Street.

When he got to Blair Street, he turned left toward the Placer Hole. There were a lot of men on the street, most of them silver miners, out to gamble, meet women, see old friends, tell stories, hear news, and get drunk. Abraham felt like one of them. After all, his father had been a miner. It was a good profession, with a lot of good men in it, and some day he might follow it. "But not now," he said to himself. "This year I'm going to do something else."

3

The doorway and the front wall of the Placer Hole didn't go together. The wall, a high clapboard square facing the street, was weak and thin and cheap. The doorway, big, dark, and carefully made, looked like the entrance to a Greek temple or a New York bank. A lot of buildings in Silverton were like that, thin walls nailed to beautiful doors.

Inside, it smelled of wet wood, kerosene, and whiskey. Abraham liked the smell. Big brass lanterns with wide wicks hung from the ceiling by chains. At the table next to the door, three men sat drinking and talking. There was a table of card players toward the back, and groups of drinkers here and there. There was a small booth against the left wall, and inside the barman was polishing glasses. Over him hung a big picture, seven or eight feet high, of a woman in a jewel-covered dress in front of a velvet curtain, singing.

Abraham walked over to the booth, hoping that he looked at least fourteen, and maybe fifteen. He counted the steps as he went. Eighteen steps from the door to the booth.

"My father gambled here once," he said when he got there. The barman, who was wearing a white shirt and a black silk vest, but no tie, said nothing.

"It was about a year ago," Abraham said.

"Win?"

"No, sir, but he didn't lose very much. Ten dollars."

"Send you here to win it back?"

"I just thought I'd like to play," Abraham said. "I'm leaving town and I wanted to do it before I left. I thought I'd play blackjack."

The barman looked at him. "You're not old enough. How much have you got?"

"Ten dollars."

The barman reached under the counter and took out a dark box. "You want to buy some cards? Five dollars, with the case. Oriental teakwood from Denver."

"No, thank you," Abraham said.

"Brand-new. Never been used, box or cards."

"No, thank you very much," Abraham said.

The barman shrugged his shoulders, put the box back under the counter, and started polishing glasses again. Abraham looked up. In her frame above the bar, the woman in the jeweled dress was still singing. He watched her for a few moments and then looked at the barman again. "Is there any place else I can go to gamble?"

The man didn't answer. Abraham felt somebody behind him and turned. Mr. Malone was standing there. "Good evening, Mr. Malone."

Mr. Malone smiled. He had a round face with bright, friendly eyes. He looked like a large baby with a beard. He spent a lot of time at the Stents' house, now that Mr. Stent and Mr. Candle were both dead, talking and acting friendly.

"Well, Abraham, what are you up to?"

"I wanted to play blackjack," Abraham said, "but I can't."

"Oh, I'm sorry," Mr. Malone said. "But that time will come. Enjoy your childhood. It'll be over soon enough."

Abraham looked at the floor and back at Mr. Malone. "I guess I have to be going. Excuse me. I'm glad to have seen you this evening, Mr. Malone."

"Where are you going?"

"I don't know." He started walking. He was going to go to the cemetery, to his father's grave. He crossed the room and went out through the door. Mr. Malone was right behind him. The sidewalk was crowded with people, and the street was crowded with burros and horses and wagons.

"Are you going home now?" Mr. Malone asked.

"In a little while."

"I want to show you something. It's on your way home. Maybe you've already seen it."

Mr. Malone started walking down Blair Street, and Abraham walked beside him. They went along for a minute or so and then, because the cemetery was the other way, Abraham stopped.

"Excuse me, Mr. Malone, but I have some business I have to do before I go back to Mrs. Stent's house."

"Oh," Mr. Malone said.

"So I'll say good evening," Abraham said.

"Is it something I can help with?" Mr. Malone asked. He looked sad and confused, like a child who has just seen his toy sailboat go over a waterfall.

Abraham shook his head. "No, thank you," he said.

"You're the most polite young man in the state of Colorado, did you know that?" Mr. Malone said. "You take after your father that way. He was the most polite, *gracious* man in the world. And he was wise, too. Some day I'll tell you some things about your father even you don't know. He was a fine man. His death was a real loss to all of us. A remarkable man."

"Thank you," Abraham said.

"Come on a few more steps with me," Mr. Malone said. "I want to show you something interesting in Finney's window. It's something you'll really be interested in. Have you already seen it? Here it is."

Finney's window had a lot of things in it: pans, ropes, sacks of coffee, nails and bolts, gloves, half a dozen hand guns hung on a chain, and twenty or thirty other different things. In the middle of the window, sitting on top of three copies of *Household Medicine: A Home Reference*, by Edwin Vegelahn, M.D., was a brown pottery jar with a squarish design running around it. Leaning against the jar was a handwritten card:

Discovered in a cave on the Mesa Verde this
AZTEK JAR
at least one thousand years of age.
Will sell.

Abraham looked at the jar. It looked like a lot of other Indian jars, except plainer.

"Every bit of that design has a special meaning. Each touch of the brush," Mr. Malone said. "If only we could read it today! How many hidden mysteries would be revealed. What an adventure it would be to go out to the Mesa Verde and find one like that, or better."

Abraham kept looking at the jar. He wanted to say something about it, but nothing came to him. It was a thousand years old. He had seen a 108-year-old Indian once. At least they said he was 108 years old. He was buying supplies in a store. He couldn't speak English, so he just pointed to what he wanted and mumbled to himself in his own language. Now that was something, to be born in 1785 and still be alive in 1893, to have your children and your grandchildren die of old age before you. But a jar, safe in a cave, why shouldn't it get to be a thousand years old, or two thousand, or three thousand?

"Mr. Finney turned down a lot of money for that jar even before he put it in the window," Mr. Malone said, leaning over Abraham's shoulder. "In Denver, that one jar alone would bring eighty dollars today. And I know where I can get twenty more, at least, most of them bigger and better. Even at only fifty dollars apiece, that would be a thousand dollars. There was a Swede out at the mesa two years ago. He took home a wagonload, and he didn't know a lot of the caves my friend knows. He knows them all."

Abraham wondered what friend Mr. Malone was talking about, but he didn't want to ask.

"And think what it would mean," he went on, "if we could find out what the symbols on all those jars meant. Then we'd have something. The money wouldn't matter." He smiled again. "You don't want to gamble at the Placer Hole. That's not what you want to do. You want to bet yourself on something bigger."

"That certainly is interesting, Mr. Malone."

"I'm glad to hear you say that, Abraham. I really am glad to hear you say it."

"But I think I'll have to go now, if you'll excuse me." Abraham backed off and turned away.

"A boy who can climb like you could get down in those caves, if he knew where they were, and get those things out in no time," Mr. Malone said as he moved off.

Abraham didn't answer. He wanted to get away from Mr. Malone. He wanted to get out of Silverton, soon and alone. He started walking faster.

4

Abraham had been to the cemetery in the dark before, so he had no trouble finding his father's grave, half way up the hill on the right-hand side. It had a high, white stone.

JOHN ALBERT CANDLE
b. Dec 12, 1831; d. Dec 29, 1892
"For I have seen God face to face"
Genesis 32:30

Abraham had wanted a plain stone, with no words on it, just his father's name and dates, but Mrs. Stent persuaded him to let the stonecutter put a scripture text on it. The bill for the stone was $25.80, including ninety cents apiece for the words.

Abraham sat down, leaned his back against the gravestone, and thought about money. He had, at the moment, $63.38 in the cigar box that he and his father had used as a bank. That was $15.28 more than when his father died. Abraham was satisfied with that. It meant that for a year and a half he had been making enough money to keep himself going without touching his reserves.

There was one big expense ahead, a winter coat. He'd have to go into the box for that. Otherwise, he could go on living on what he made alone. "Maybe," he said to himself, "if I'm in Old Mexico next winter, I won't need a coat."

He looked down at the grave, and thought about death, and remembered a story.

Once upon a time, his father said once, *there was a man named Nicholas who set out from his home to find a job in the world. He traveled here and there, from city to city, doing different jobs, meeting different people, talking and listening. Everywhere, people told him about Labor and Sickness and Death. If it weren't for Labor and Sickness and Death, they said, life would be wonderful.*

So Nicholas decided that he ought to try to rid the world of Labor and Sickness and Death. He devised a plan. He would make a strong lock, and then he would build a log cabin far away somewhere, with a heavy door on it and no windows, and then he would put his lock on the door, and then he would get Labor and Sickness and Death to come inside, and then he would lock them up, and the world would be rid of them.

So he went to a very good locksmith, and he told the locksmith his plan, and asked him if he could work for him and learn his trade.

"You can work for me, and learn my trade, but you can't hold Death and Labor and Sickness with a lock," the locksmith said. "It's impossible."

"Then I'll use more than one lock," Nicholas said. "I'll use seven locks, each one twice as good as the last."

The locksmith shook his head. "You can't hold Death and Labor and Sickness any place for long," he said.

"Maybe yes, and maybe no," Nicholas said. "But even if I could only keep them away from everybody for two minutes, it would be a good life's work."

The locksmith smiled. "You're crazy," he said, "but come on, I'll teach you what I know."

So Nicholas began working for the locksmith, and he worked for him for many years, until he knew everything the locksmith knew. Then he said goodbye, took the money he had saved, and went far into the woods, where he built a cabin with a heavy door and no windows. There, by the daylight that came in through the open door, he began working on his seven locks, each one different from the one before, and twice as strong.

From the first to the last light of day, Labor was an almost constant companion. He had known Labor for a long time, of course, and thought of him as a friend.

Half way through the making of the fifth lock, Sickness came to visit him, striking him in one eye and stiffening his hands.

"I'm not sorry to see you," he said, looking at Sickness with his better eye. "I suppose Death will come along after a while too, and then we'll all be in the cabin together."

"You look forward to Death's visit?" Sickness asked.

"When I'm through with my work," Nicholas said.

"No one looks forward to Death," Sickness said, "not even an old man like you."

Nicholas smiled, and went on working.

More years passed, and Sickness came to visit more and more often, and stayed longer each time, walking back and forth in the room with a restless, nervous look on his face, or standing, hunched over, staring at the locks.

Finally all seven locks were finished and Nicholas set them, one above the other, in the door. Then, leaving the door open, he took a long walk into town and had a glass of beer to celebrate. He drank it slowly, enjoying it so much that he had another. Then he walked back into the woods to his cabin. Inside he saw Death waiting for him, with Sickness on one side and Labor on the other.

He pretended not to see them, but slowly closed the door, and in the darkness of the cabin he locked the seven locks, one by one, each in its own special way. Then he turned around.

"Welcome," he said, "especially to you, Death, whom

I have not had the pleasure of meeting before. As you know, Sir, Labor and Sickness and I are old friends. Shall I lie down on my bed, first, or do you prefer to kill me where I stand?"

"You are very kind to welcome me," Death said, "and I thank you for it."

"I want you to feel at home here," Nicholas said.

"Thank you again."

Sickness sneezed twice. Then Nicholas heard him scratching himself in the dark.

"Light a candle," Sickness said. "I think I'm getting a rash."

"May I, Death?" Nicholas asked. "I know you can see perfectly well in the dark, but Sickness seems to be having some trouble."

"Go ahead," Death said. "I don't mind at all."

Nicholas took a match out of his pocket, struck it, and lit a candle. Sickness had a rash all over his left arm. He didn't look well at all. Death didn't pay any attention to him but looked directly at Nicholas. "Before I take you," he said, "I wonder if you'd mind opening the door. I have many calls to make tonight and, as you know, Labor and Sickness have their work to do, too."

"Forgive me, Death," Nicholas said, "but that is the one thing I will not do."

Death looked at him soberly and seriously, while Sickness went on scratching. "I hate to be closed in a room," Sickness said. "I need some fresh air."

Death still paid Sickness no attention but kept look-

ing directly at Nicholas. "Labor and I together will soon enough be able to unlock your locks," he said. "You might as well do it for us and save us the trouble."

Nicholas said nothing, and Death and Labor went to the door and started working on the first lock. In a few seconds it clattered to the floor, and they started working on the second one. That lock took a little more time, but soon it too clattered to the floor.

"Hurry up," Sickness said. He was walking back and forth now, scratching himself. He had a nasty-looking rash on both arms. Death and Labor paid no attention to him. They were having some trouble with the third lock. Nicholas went over to the door and watched them. They worked together well. Labor was quick-handed and strong, and Death was always thinking and planning far ahead. Nicholas admired the way they worked. The third lock fell, and Death looked at him and smiled.

"Four to go," he said.

Nicholas watched and watched and watched. The candle on the table burned down and went out. The darkness didn't bother Nicholas or Labor or Death, but Sickness almost went crazy in the dark. He jumped and screamed and kicked so much that Nicholas, out of pity for him, lit another candle.

The fourth lock fell. Now Sickness, red with fever, knocked Death and Labor aside and started pushing and scratching on the fifth lock, but he was no good at it. He stopped and looked at Nicholas. "Revenge on you, old man! Plague! Plague! Revenge and plague!" he screamed. Nicholas stared back at him, not so much afraid as amazed. Death reached out and took Sickness by the wrist.

"Leave the good man alone," he said. "He's mine now, not yours."

Nicholas felt sorry for Sickness. He had never seen anyone so tormented. "You can lie down on my bed if you'd like," he said to him. "I'll bring you a glass of water."

This offer made the wretched creature more violent than ever, and he screamed and fell on the floor. Nicholas, with nothing else to do, went to his bed and lay down. In spite of the noise, he immediately fell asleep.

He slept a long time, a peaceful, dreamless, and beautiful sleep, and he would have slept longer if Death had not come to his bed and called his name.

"Nicholas," he said, "we're almost done with the seventh lock."

"How long did I keep you working?" Nicholas asked.

"Twelve hours."

Nicholas was glad to hear that.

"Labor and I are going now," Death said, "and we're taking our friend Sickness with us. We'll keep him until he recovers."

Death went to the door, where Labor stood with Sickness thrown over his shoulder, tied up in a sack with only his head showing. Then he turned around and looked at Nicholas again. "You are under my protection," he said. "In time, I will come for you again. Until then, enjoy your good health."

Labor touched the seventh lock. It fell, and the door opened, and they went out. It was morning. The sun was rising, and Nicholas felt refreshed.

On strong legs, with clear eyes, he set out for the city, hating Sickness with all his heart, but not afraid of him, and glad to have seen Death and found him to be a serious and honorable person.

Abraham stood up and looked across the cemetery toward the town. There was a glow over Blair Street, like the glow over a fire in a pit. He looked down at his father's grave.

"I wish you were here," he said quietly.

He thought of the Great McGregor on top of his mountain bending over to take a drink, and of the mysterious woman saying, "If you drink, you die." He shook his head. His father would never have made up a character like the Great McGregor. He might have made up the Foolish McGregor, or the Blue McGregor, or the McGregor-with-a-Face-Like-a-Walnut, but he never would have made up the Great McGregor.

"I wish you weren't dead," he said.

At the time of his father's death the cemetery keeper had offered to sell him enough ground for four graves, but he had said no. There was no one else in the family, so why spend extra money? Now his father's grave was surrounded by the graves of strangers. Friedrich Schumacher on his left, Ernest White on his right, and Elizabeth Tree Gaines, beloved wife of Thomas L. Gaines, at his feet. That was fine. It gave the cemetery dignity to have a lot of graves in it, close together but not crowded. It was a good cemetery to be buried in.

"Goodbye," Abraham said. He stepped carefully across the grave of Ernest White and started down the slope toward the entrance, a high iron gate fifty or sixty graves away. He thought of Mr. Malone telling him he wanted to bet himself on something big. The man was wrong. He didn't want to bet anything on anything. He wanted to change, to grow older, and wiser, and better, and he wanted to do it soon.

And, if possible, he wanted it to show on his face.

5

When he got home, Mrs. Stent was sitting at the kitchen table having a cup of coffee. He sat down across from her.

"Where were you, Abraham?"

"On Blair Street, at the Placer Hole."

"Did you have a good time?"

"Yes, thank you."

"Would you like a cup of coffee?"

"Yes, please." He got up.

"Sit down," she said. "I'll get it for you."

He sat back down, and she went to the stove.

"Jane woke up five minutes after you left. She kept calling you. I told her you were gone and you wouldn't be back until later, but she wouldn't listen. She just kept calling 'Abram, Abram, Abram'—you know how she says your name—until she cried herself to sleep. Then Robie said you didn't kiss him good night, so he couldn't go to sleep either."

"I did kiss him good night."

"That's what I told him. I told him I saw you do it, but you know how he is. We've always gotten along well together, haven't we, Abraham?"

"Yes, we have, Mrs. Stent," he said. He wondered what she wanted. He paid $22 a month for a dark room, three terrible meals a day, and a glass of oat milk every night. Now what did she want from him? And she still hadn't poured him his cup of coffee.

She smiled and came back from the stove, sat down and leaned toward him. "If your father hadn't passed away, the two of us would have gotten married, don't you think so?"

Abraham didn't answer.

"I know you two men were very close. I see him in you every day. He was a remarkable man, Abraham. You've grown up a lot the last year. I've been watching you, and I'm proud of it.

"And you're smart, really smart. Mrs. Graham told me last week that you were the best and most courteous student she's ever had. And you're much more grown up than most boys your age, even the ones already working to help care for large families."

She stood up and leaned across the table and kissed

him on the cheek, getting hair in his face. Suddenly Abraham knew what she wanted. "She's going to ask me to marry her," he said to himself. "She's going to ask me to marry her." He began quickly to figure out how to say no without being rude, while she kept talking to him about what a wonderful young man he was.

"You don't know how young I really am," he would say. "I still want to hear somebody tell me stories. I'm very young. You can't depend on me. I'm just about to leave town. Anyway, it wouldn't be legal."

This last thought made him feel better. He was, really, too young. He was even too young to gamble. But what if she planned to keep him around for two or three more years and then marry him? She might have that in mind. Get him to stay for the sake of the children, let them begin calling him Poppy or something, and then stick him in two or three years. He'd heard of marriages like that. Up at the Lucky Girl Mine there was a sixteen-year-old boy who married a widow almost fifty. But it wasn't going to happen to him. Not for anything. He was going away. Tomorrow, probably. Yes, that was a good idea. He'd go away tomorrow.

He looked up and realized that Mrs. Stent had stopped talking. Had she already asked him to marry her, and he wasn't listening? Was she waiting for his answer? She smiled.

"We're good friends, aren't we, Abraham? Really good friends."

"Yes, Mrs. Stent, we are."

"Maybe you'd like to go away on a trip, and then come back. You've got a good home here."

She stopped and looked at him with a serious face. "Mr. Malone came by to visit this evening, and he was saying that you look a little restless. Why don't the two of you go away for a little while? What would you think of that?"

"Well," Abraham said, "I don't know."

"I'd feel much better, if the two of you went together. The children and I can get along until you come back. You don't need to think about us. A boy ought to get away for a little adventure. Your father told me that once."

"I don't know," Abraham said. He looked down at the table and then back at Mrs. Stent. "Maybe if I left I might decide, for some reason, not to come back. That might happen."

Mrs. Stent shook her head, looked sad, and smiled, and Abraham suddenly felt sorry for her. In a strange and small way, he loved her. "Maybe I ought to marry her," he said to himself. "Then I could set this house right. It's too much to leave her with Robie and Julie. They walk all over her."

He stood up. "I guess I'll go to bed," he said. "Are you going to bed, Mrs. Stent?"

"You want some coffee?" she asked.

"No, thank you," Abraham said. "Maybe tomorrow morning, thank you."

• • •

A few minutes later, he was lying on his back in the darkness of his room, thinking. He saw in his mind the mountains crowding close to the house. In one corner of the mountains there was a crack, with light coming through it. Beyond that crack was Durango, and Texas, and the Gulf of Mexico, and the whole world.

He tried to see himself in one of those places, to imagine himself as a man, with a place, and a job, and a certain kind of face, but he couldn't do it. He couldn't even decide whether his face should have a beard on it or not. Mr. Malone had a beard, but on the other hand so did Abraham Lincoln. All kinds of people had beards. There was no way to decide.

Lincoln said that a man was responsible for his own face after he got to be forty. Before then, he could blame it on his parents or other people, but after forty he had to answer for it himself. "Ugly children take courage, and beautiful children beware," Abraham's father said once, "because you have forty years to work on your faces and get them finished."

6

The next morning Abraham got up early and went down to the railroad station to make some money unpacking burros. A man who owned his own mine, or shared a claim with two or three partners, never hired anybody to help him. He had led his animals a long way over hard trails, and he owed it to himself and his partners to unload every sack of ore himself and be with it when it was weighed and tallied. It was hard on the animal at the end of the train, having to stand under a hundred-pound pack waiting his turn, but it was a rare miner who cared so much for his burros that he'd let a stranger help unpack them.

With the company mines it was different. Their ore was packed in by hired men who were glad to get somebody to do their job for them, if his price was low enough. Abraham's price was thirty-five cents a train, and on a good day he could work five or six trains.

It was a simple enough job. Beginning with the first burro in line, he would untie the pack and carry the ore, two sacks at a time, to the scales on the loading platform. As each burro was unpacked, Abraham would take him out of line, coil his ropes, roll his pack blanket, lead him away, and tie him with the others to a post on the freight-house wall. That way, when all of them had been unpacked and all the ore had been weighed and samples of it assayed and the company credited, the packer would find all his burros together in one place waiting for him.

The first pack train came into the station yard a little after Abraham got there. It was a company train, and the packer was glad to pay him thirty-five cents to unload it. After that there was another, and Abraham worked all day long. Late in the afternoon he took his sixth job, and when he had been paid he decided he had enough time to take a swim. The Stents always ate late.

A quarter of a mile south of town, where the railroad turned left across the Animas River and started into the canyon, there was a big cold pond. Nobody ever swam there because it looked like a swamp and was full of muskrats, but Abraham liked it. It was his own place. He didn't bother the muskrats, and the muskrats didn't bother him.

He walked down the railroad tracks until he got to

the pond, went down the bank, took off his clothes, and flopped into the cold water. For the next half hour he patrolled the pond back and forth, watching the small dark heads that moved from one shore to the other, watching him.

When his patrolling was over, he got out of the water, shook himself off, and picked up his suit of underwear. It was damp with his sweat and it stank, so he threw it in the pond, went in after it, and rubbed and squeezed and pulled it back and forth until his arms were tired. Then he got out again, wrung the underwear out, folded it up, put on his pants and shirt and socks and shoes, and started home with his underwear under his arm.

When he got to the Stents', he hung it on a tree in the back yard and went into the kitchen. Mr. Malone was there, sitting at the table with a cup of coffee. Robie and Julie were in the front room fighting over something. Jane was sitting on the floor behind her mother. She got up and came over to him. He picked her up.

"Good evening, Mrs. Stent. Mr. Malone."

Mrs. Stent smiled. "Welcome home, Abraham. Did you have a nice day? What can those children be fighting about in there?"

"I'm glad to see you again, Abraham," Mr. Malone said.

"I'm glad to see you too, sir," Abraham lied. "Julie, come in the kitchen and set the table. Dinner's almost ready."

"Robie hid my button box," Julie shouted.

"I did not," Robie yelled. "She's got my laces."

"Julie," Abraham said, his voice louder but still calm, "set the table."

She came in. "He's got my button box," she said. Robie didn't follow her in, so Abraham guessed that she was telling the truth.

"Set the table," he said. "I'll talk to him after dinner."

Dinner was better than usual: sliced beef, salty but hot; boiled potatoes, beans, and coffee. While they ate, Mr. Malone talked of his past. His father, who had left his mother to fight in the Civil War and not come back, had been cold and mean. His mother, the youngest of five sisters, had been warm and sweet, but not strong. When he was seventeen he had found comfort in the study of civil engineering. At eighteen, he left for the West to learn a trade. Since that time he had been a carpenter in Nyack, New York; a bookseller in Philadelphia, Pennsylvania; an organ builder in Baltimore, Maryland; and a wheel fitter in a wagon factory in Kansas City, Missouri.

"Do you know what all my experiences have taught me?" he asked. "I've found out that a person can find truth in everything, if he has the eyes to see it, and if he's willing to go a little out of his way sometimes."

"I'm sure you're right, Thornton," Mrs. Stent said.

• • •

Dinner took a long time. After it was over, Mrs. Stent and Julie washed the dishes and Abraham got the button box back from Robie. Then the children put on their nightshirts and went into the kitchen for their oat milk.

"What happened to the Great McGregor?" Robie asked. "After that woman told him not to drink."

Abraham didn't have a chance to answer. Mr. Malone spoke first.

"Maybe tonight I could tell a story," he said. "What would you think of that?"

"Abraham already has a story," Julie said.

"My story is called 'The Secret Treasure,'" Mr. Malone went on. "I think you'll really enjoy it."

No one said anything, so he started.

"Once upon a time, long ago, there was an old Indian tribe here in Colorado that was dying out, and the Indian chief didn't know what to do. So he went to the Medicine Man, who was very old and very wise, and said to him, 'What must we do, now that our tribe is dying out?' Well, the Medicine Man started right away to pray to the Great Spirit, and after a long time of praying very deeply—because you need to do that, you know, to have a prayer truly answered—the Great Spirit answered him and told him exactly what they ought to do."

Mr. Malone looked at Robie very earnestly. "It's an exciting story, isn't it? Stories about Indians are always exciting. You want to know what happened after that?"

"What happened?" Robie asked.

"Well, the Great Spirit said to the Medicine Man, which the Medicine Man told the Chief, 'Yes, it is true, your tribe is dying out. There is only one thing you must do. You must take all your wisdom and all your sacred signs and put them on pottery and hide them from your enemies. Then you can die in peace.'

" 'Since it is the will of the gods, I will do it,' said the Chief.

"So they painted all their sacred signs and all their wisdom on pottery and hid it in caves not very far from this very spot, and many centuries passed. In 1492 Columbus discovered America. Soon the Spaniards under Cortez came up from Old Mexico. Finally, the American Race came, bringing Civilization, Churches, Schools, Free Commerce, and the Blessings of Liberty, but the wisdom of the Indians remained hidden, guarded by the Great Spirit."

Jane climbed down from Abraham's lap and went into the front room. Abraham got up to follow her.

"Don't go," Mr. Malone said. "Mrs. Stent will put her to bed, won't you, Pauline?"

Mrs. Stent got up and went into the front room, and Abraham sat back down to listen to the rest of the story.

"Well," Mr. Malone said, "then something happened. There was a boy who lived near where the caves with the pottery were, a brave boy who could climb very well and was very adventurous. He went down into the caves with two friends, and there, in the caves, he found the ancient vases, and together he and his friends studied the symbols on them and discovered what they meant and brought the Indian wisdom back to civilization and shared it with their fellow men."

Mr. Malone stopped, and everybody was quiet for about half a minute. Then Robie spoke. "What happened after that?"

"They lived happily ever after," Mr. Malone said.

"Oh," Robie said.

Abraham watched him and felt disappointed. Sure, it was a stupid story and Mr. Malone didn't tell it very well and he only told it to persuade Abraham to go to the mesa with him, but the idea behind the story, the idea of finding something valuable and bringing it to mankind, was a good idea, and Abraham was sorry that Robie didn't seem to see that.

Mr. Malone looked at him. "What do you think of the story, Abraham?" he asked.

"I like the idea behind it," Abraham said.

"Good. I'm glad to hear that. Maybe it's just too grown up a story for Robie and Julie to understand and appreciate fully."

Julie leaned toward Abraham. "What about your story?"

Abraham shrugged. "I don't know what happens next."

Julie looked shocked. "You don't?"

"No. But I'll think about it tonight or tomorrow, and then I'll tell you. It's almost the end now. It's the last chapter coming up. Now you ought to go to bed."

Julie complained, and so did Robie, but Abraham insisted, so they went, and soon afterward he said good night, got ready for bed, went into his room and went to sleep.

After what seemed like a very short time, he woke up to find Mr. Malone standing next to his bed with a lantern in his hand.

"Abraham?"

"Hello, Mr. Malone."

"Are you awake, Abraham?"

He thought for a second. "Yes."

"There's somebody I want you to meet. You don't have to get dressed. Nobody will see you."

Abraham sat up. "Who is it?"

"Are you awake?"

"Who is it?"

"A very interesting person."

"Oh." Abraham swung his legs out of bed. "Where is he?"

"In the front. I want you to meet him."

Mr. Malone led the way through the house. The front door was open. Outside, it was still and cold and clear. Standing in the middle of the yard was a tall man dressed in dark work clothes, with his left arm in a leather sling. "I want you two to meet," Mr. Malone said. "Abraham, this is Mr. Green. Mr. Green, this is Abraham Candle."

"It's a pleasure to meet you, Mr. Green," Abraham said.

"Mr. Green will be going with us to the mesa—if we go, that is," Mr. Malone said.

Abraham nodded. His feet were cold.

"You'll catch your death of cold out here," Mr. Malone said. "We'd better go in."

"That's a good idea," Abraham said. "Good night, Mr. Green. It was a pleasure making your acquaintance." He turned and walked back into the house, with Mr. Malone behind him. He went into his room and got back into bed, and Mr. Malone came into the room after him, carrying the lantern.

"Dark in here, isn't it?" Mr. Malone said.

"You can turn up the lantern if you want," Abraham said.

Mr. Malone turned it up and sat down on the end of the bed. "What do you think, Abraham—do you want to go with us? We really need you, you know. You're such a wonderful climber, and you're strong." He smiled. "We also need a little money. I'm going to put in a little, but we need a little more. You have to invest a little money if you're going to make any."

Abraham thought for a minute. "I have $65.48," he said then. "I could put in fifty dollars."

"Is that all? I thought you had more."

"No. When are you going?"
"Pretty soon."
"Tomorrow?"
"Well, maybe."
"Let's go tomorrow," Abraham said. "I can go ahead, if you're not ready, and you can catch up with me."
Mr. Malone didn't like that idea. "I think we can all go tomorrow," he said. "I'll go tell Mr. Green."
He walked out, leaving the room in darkness, and Abraham turned over and went to sleep.

7

When Abraham got up the next morning, he went to the trunk and got out his father's working shoes. They were medium high, coming up to a little above the ankles, with hard, thick soles and heels. His father had paid eight dollars for them second-hand. "All a man really needs," he said to Abraham once, "is good shoes, good socks, good underwear, and good gloves. Everything else is decoration."

Abraham got on his clothes and tried the shoes. They fit fine. He kept them on and got some other things out of his trunk: socks, his other suit of underwear, two shirts, two sweaters, a long, narrow waterproof tarp, a blanket, and two short pieces of rope.

He laid everything on the blanket, folded it over twice, rolled it up, and tied it. He was ready to travel.

He went into the kitchen, ate two oatcakes with blackberry butter, and went out of the house quietly by the back door. In his right pants pocket was a leather pouch with $65.48 in it. He went to the tailor shop, which opened early, and bought ten dollars' worth of white silk. In case he didn't ever come back to Silverton, he wanted Jane to be able to make something beautiful for herself some day.

He went back to the house, wrote *Jane Stent* on the package of silk, and put it in his trunk. Then he went down to the train station and spent the morning at the loading platform helping packers. It wasn't what he wanted to do. He wanted just to buy a ticket for Durango and sit around listening to the miners talk. But one of the company packers saw him and asked him to help, and then two more jobs came along. When he left the station, he had $1.05 in his pocket to add to his $55.48.

On the way home he saw Mr. Green on the other side of the street. He was walking slowly and carefully, so that Abraham knew he was drunk. His left arm was still in its leather sling. Mr. Green looked at him, but didn't recognize him.

When Abraham got to the house, Mr. Malone was there, with Jane sitting on his lap eating a sea biscuit. The children were out, and Mrs. Stent was upstairs resting. Abraham and Mr. Malone said very little to each other. They ate some lentil soup and bread. Abraham gave Mr. Malone fifty dollars, and they agreed to meet at the station at five. Then Abraham went out to hunt for the children. He wanted very much to talk to them about Jane.

He found them building a hut in a place near the cave.

"I want to talk to you about something," he said.

"What?" Julie asked.

"I'm going away this afternoon. I'm not sure when I'll come back."

"Ma says you'll be back in a few weeks," Robie said.

"Maybe I will. I don't know, I can't tell."

"If you don't come back in a few weeks, when will you come back?" Julie asked.

"I don't know," Abraham said. "Maybe things'll work out so I don't come back at all."

The children were shocked. "You can't do that, not come back," Julie said. "You live with us."

"I lived with you when my father was alive," Abraham said, "and since he died. But maybe I ought to be going some place else now. Your mother could rent the room to somebody else. There'd be somebody around. And Mr. Malone will be coming back."

Robie started to say "I don't like him," but Abraham put his hand over the boy's mouth.

"I don't think you ought to go at all," Julie said. "Why do you have to?"

Abraham looked at her, but he didn't answer. "I want

to talk to you about Jane," he said. "She's still a baby, you know, and sometimes you treat her mean."

"I don't do anything," Julie said.

"Neither do I," Robie said.

"She needs somebody to hold her once in a while," Abraham said, "and be with her and tell her a story once in a while."

"She's awful young for stories," Robie said.

"No, she isn't," Abraham said. "Nobody's too young for stories. Even when you don't understand a story, it's good to be told it. She likes *any* stories. It's good for her. And listen. There's a package in my trunk that belongs to her. It's a birthday present for when she's twelve years old."

"Is there anything in there for us?" Robie asked.

"No, but if I don't come back, I'll send you something in the mail."

"I don't think you should go," Julie said.

Abraham stood up. "The train leaves at five. You going to come to the station?"

"Sure," Robie said.

"Then come down to the house pretty soon. You can go with your mother, if she goes." Abraham started back toward town. He wanted to get his blanket roll and go down to the pond and watch the muskrats for a while.

The winter his father died, Abraham told Julie and Robie a story they didn't like or understand at all. It was one of his father's stories, and he told it the way he remembered his father telling it, but they didn't understand it.

Once upon a time, far far away, there was a man named Richard who lived in the country. One morning Richard sat up in bed and said to his Soul, "Soul, I believe I will go to town today and visit my brother John and do him a kindness, and I will take you along, because only a fool would go to town to do his brother a kindness and leave his Soul at home."

So he took his right shoe out from under the bed, put his Soul in it, and put it on. Then he put on the rest of his clothes and left.

"He put his Soul in his shoe?" Robie said.

"Why not, if that's where he wanted to put it?" Julie said.

Robie shut his mouth, and Abraham went on with the story.

Well, it was a long walk to his brother's house, and it was dark by the time he got there. He knocked, and his brother opened the door.

"Hello, Richard!" his brother said. "What do you want?"

"I thought I'd do you a kindness, if I can," Richard said.

"Like what?"

"I don't know."

"How about digging me a well?"

"Good," Richard said. He sat down, took off his right shoe, and took his Soul out of it. "Would you mind holding my Soul for me while I'm digging?" he asked. "I've been walking on it all day, and I don't want to be stamping on it all night."

"That's not your Soul," John said. "That's a rock."

"See, I told you, you can't put your Soul in a shoe," Robie said.

Julie punched him in the arm. "I didn't say you could put your Soul in a shoe," she said. "That's stupid."

Robie punched her back. "You did too."

She punched him back. "I did not."

"Stop it," Abraham said. "My father made up this story, so stop hitting each other and listen."

So Richard's brother said, "That's not your Soul, it's a rock."

Richard was silent for a minute. "John," he said then, "you're right. I wonder where my Soul is."

"The same place it always is," his brother said. "Same place everybody's is."

Richard shook his head. "No," he said. "It moved when I spoke to it this morning. It was on top of that rock, and when I told it where I was going, it went."

"Don't worry about it," his brother said. "You'll find it."

"Where's yours?" Richard asked.

"Around," John said. "Now, are you going to dig that well for me, or are you just going to sit there asking questions?"

So Richard took his other shoe off, picked up the lantern, went out, picked up a shovel, brought it around in front, and started to dig. In a little while he was down to gravel, and with the first light of morning he struck water. It flowed in, cool and clear, until it was up to his waist, and then he saw a trout swimming around in it with his Soul on its tail. "Soul," he said, "I sure am glad to see you. How did you get here? If I hadn't dug this well, I never would have found you. Well, I am glad to see you, and that is a fact." He leaned back against the side of the well, put his hands behind his head, watched the fish and waited for his brother to come.

"I don't get it," Robie said. "How did his Soul get onto the fish?"

"Because it went to the place where he was going to go to do the good deed," Abraham said. "He told his Soul he was going there, and it went there."

"Why?"

"Because Souls are like that," Julie said. "Don't you know anything?"

"Both of you be quiet," Abraham said.

Finally, Richard's brother came with a ladder.

"Hello, John," Richard said when he was out. "I found my Soul. It's down there on the tail of a fish. A trout."

"You're crazy," John said. "If it's anybody's Soul down there, it's mine," John said.

"How long has your Soul been gone?" Richard asked.

"It's not gone," John said. "I always keep it in the same place. When are you leaving?"

"I could leave now," Richard said.

"That's a good idea," John said.

So Richard turned around and looked down into the well. "Soul?" he called. The trout popped his head out of the water. "I'm going home now and cook some dinner."

When he looked up, John was standing on the porch with a fishing pole. "You don't happen to know where any worms are, by any chance, do you?" he asked.

"I don't think so," Richard said, "unless one got into my pocket during the night." He reached into his pocket, and there was a worm. "I found one," he said, and handed it to his brother.

"Thanks again," John said. "Well, goodbye."

"Goodbye," Richard said, and walked away. When he got outside of town, he stepped on a sharp rock. "Ow!" he said, jumping up and down. "I forgot to take my shoes." So he turned around and started back toward the house. But when he got near it, he saw his brother sitting on the front porch fishing in the well. "I wonder what he's trying to catch?" Richard asked himself. "Is he trying to catch my Soul, or his Soul, or that trout? Well, whatever it is, it would be a sin to disturb him just for a pair of shoes. I'll leave him alone."

So Richard went home barefoot, looking forward to seeing his Soul again, probably on top of his stove.

And that's the end of the story.

"Why did he let his brother keep ahold of his shoes?" Robie asked. "Didn't he care about his shoes?"

Abraham didn't answer. Instead he got up, put on his sheepskin coat, and went out to look at the ice on Muskrat Pond.

As he left the house, Robie and Julie started fighting again.

Abraham spent a lot of time that winter looking at the pond. Now it was a year and a half later, and he was looking at it for what might be the last time. He sat down on the bank and watched the muskrats.

"I told my Soul last night I was going to the mesa," he said to himself after a while, "so now it's there waiting for me. I wonder how often it happens that a man says he's going to go some place, and his Soul hears him and goes there, and then the man doesn't go, and forgets, and loses his Soul and never gets it back, and doesn't even know it's gone."

He watched the muskrats swim across the pond and around behind a clump of grass. It felt like it was getting close to five. He climbed up the bank and looked the half mile down the tracks toward the station. The train was in, blowing steam up into the air, and there were some people gathered around it. He started walking slowly in that direction.

Half way there Abraham saw all the Stents, and Mr. Malone and Mr. Green, standing next to the passenger car, waiting for him. He didn't hurry to get to them. Why should he? He was the climber. They could do without Mr. Green. And they could do without Mr. Malone. But they couldn't do without him. He was the one necessary man. With him, they would get treasure. Without him, they might just as well not go.

Robie saw him and started running toward him, and Julie came right behind. They came to the end of the low station platform and jumped off and ran along the tracks side by side. They banged into him at about the same time.

"Who won?" Robie shouted.

"I won," Julie said. "You had a head start."

"I did not," Robie said. "I won, didn't I, Abraham?"

"It was a tie," Abraham said, looking at the end of the platform. Jane was standing there, crying. "You shouldn't have left Jane. She could get lost or hurt or something following you."

"Ma was holding her hand," Julie said. "Robie was the one who started running first."

Abraham got to the platform, picked up Jane, and kept walking until he got to where Mrs. Stent and Mr. Malone and Mr. Green were.

"I bought the tickets," Mr. Malone said with a hearty

smile, "so we're all ready to go. In three days, or four at the most, we'll be on the Mesa Verde."

The engine gave three short whistles. Mrs. Stent's eyes got bigger. "It's leaving," she said.

Abraham shook his head. "That's just the signal for backing up."

"Oh," she said. "Well, you know best." Abraham looked at Mr. Green. His arm was still in its leather sling. He didn't look very drunk, only sad. Abraham squeezed Jane tighter. He wanted to take her with him, to have someone to talk to and play cards with. "I'll write you a letter," he said quietly in her ear. "Your mother can read it to you, all right?"

She didn't answer. She was too busy looking at the engine, which was blowing steam into the air.

"Be careful, Abraham," Mrs. Stent said.

"You didn't finish the Great McGregor," Julie said, "so you owe us."

"I won't forget," Abraham said. The station agent came out of his house and crossed the platform. "I guess we'd better get on."

He kissed Jane again and handed her to Mrs. Stent. Mr. Malone put his arms around mother and child and patted them both. The engine whistled its ready signal, and Mr. Green led the way toward the passenger car, carrying Mr. Malone's suitcase. The goodbyes got noisy. Jane started to scream. Robie took hold of Abraham's hand, so that he had to pull it away, and the train started moving. They got on. The last person Abraham heard was Mrs. Stent. "Remember your father!" she called out to him.

He knew what she meant. She meant please come back.

Part II

8

It was a beautiful railroad car. At each end there was a stove, a bin of coal, a small shovel, an enclosed toilet, and a water cooler with a brass cup. The middle aisle had a red carpet on it, and the window frames, walls, and ceilings were made of polished mahogany and ash wood. Every seat had a window.

Abraham looked out at the Animas River, running clear and fast near the tracks. Above the river the mountains slid slowly by—Sultan, Grand Turk, and the Great Needles, with plains of snow near their peaks. Lower down there were trails, mine entrances, shaft houses, and shacks, most of them empty.

After a while Abraham fell asleep, and when he woke up it was twilight outside and the conductor was coming down the aisle lighting the lamps. Mr. Green's reflection slowly appeared in the window glass. He was sitting absolutely still, his eyes staring at the stove at the end of the car. What was he thinking? He sat so completely silent and still. "Some day," Abraham said to himself, "I'll find out about him."

He began thinking about his Great McGregor story. The Great McGregor was up the mountain and Elizabeth and Freemont were down in the cave with the Octopus. Who was the woman who warned him not to drink the water? The Great McGregor's mother? His sister? A goddess of some sort? The Black Octopus in disguise? Abraham stopped. He liked the idea. Yes. That's who she was. She was the Black Octopus in disguise, trying to keep the Great McGregor away from the water so that he would become weak and die. Of course, the Great McGregor wouldn't be fooled. He'd come over to her, pretending not to recognize her, and then he'd grab her and tie her up and carry her on his shoulders down to the cave and rescue the children. No, he'd *have a drink* and then grab her and tie her and carry her on his shoulders down to the cave and rescue the children.

And he'd leave her there in chains, and Elizabeth and Freemont would promise never to go exploring again without the permission of their parents.

The end.

Great. Wonderful. Now he had his last chapter. He was ready to see the children again, if he had to.

He imagined himself going back to Silverton on the train. He could see Mrs. Stent and the children as he came around the last bend into town. The children began waving. He waved back. Under his left arm he carried a large Indian jar wrapped in tissue paper. It was a beautiful jar, very large and very fragile, with strange designs painted all around it.

It was the most important Indian jar that had ever been found on the North American continent.

He saw himself getting off the train. He shook hands with Mrs. Stent and picked up Jane with one arm while he kept the jar in the other. Jane kissed him, and Julie gave him flowers, and Robie hung on to his sleeve. "What about the story?" Robie asked.

"Tonight, when you're ready for bed," Abraham answered. "Tonight I'll tell you who the Black Octopus really is."

Abraham leaned against the window and looked out. The Animas River was still next to the train, but the mountains were now far back. In a field beyond the river he saw an elk standing very still, looking like a horse with a broken neck. A minute after the elk was out of sight, the first lights of Durango appeared.

Durango was just like Silverton, except bigger.

"We'll go to the Antrim House," Mr. Malone said as he and Mr. Green and Abraham walked away from the train.

"Where's that?" Abraham asked.

"Not far," Mr. Malone said. "It won't take us long.

You'll like Mrs. Antrim. She's a wonderful cook. She's an old friend of mine. Nothing too close, of course, but a grand person. Real pioneer stock."

In a few minutes they were at Mrs. Antrim's. She didn't seem to remember Mr. Malone, but she had rooms to rent.

"For you two and the boy?" she asked.

Mr. Malone said yes, but Abraham said no, thank you, he'd sleep in the barn if that was all right.

"Cost you ten cents," Mrs. Antrim said. "For twenty-five you can have a little room of your own. But suit yourself. You'll all three want breakfast, I suppose. That's fifteen cents. Twenty cents with pork."

Mr. Malone smiled at Mrs. Antrim and nodded, but he looked sad, and Abraham thought again how much he looked like a baby.

"I'll show you your rooms," Mrs. Antrim said, and started down the hall toward the back stairs. Mr. Green and Mr. Malone followed her. "When you're ready, come on up and see me," Mr. Malone said. "I want to have a little talk."

Abraham was hungry and he was tired and the last thing he wanted to do was have a talk with Mr. Malone. Nevertheless, after he had gone to the barn and unrolled his blanket and gone back to the railroad station and had a bowl of soup, he returned to the house, went up the stairs, and found Mr. Malone's room. The man was already in bed.

"I wish there was something here we could have to eat," Mr. Malone said.

Abraham didn't mention the soup. "Couldn't you go down to the kitchen and have a piece of bread or something?" he asked.

"Do you think I could?" Mr. Malone said. He didn't move or say anything more for about a minute.

"You wanted to talk to me about something?" Abraham asked.

"Yes," Mr. Malone said. "I want to talk to you about what we're going to do when we get to the caves on the mesa." His voice began to sound almost happy, and he stopped looking hungry. "It's going to be a great adventure, you know, Abraham, a really great adventure. We're going to get wonderful, really marvelous things, things no white man has ever seen before. The wisdom of the ages. We may even open a new chapter in human history." He leaned forward. "Mr. Green knows where it all is, and he's going to show us everything. It'll be like digging up pirate treasure, or something."

He leaned back and talked on and on and on, and as he talked Abraham had to try harder and harder to look interested. He had heard it all before. He wanted it to be true, but the childish way Mr. Malone talked made him wonder. "If he was my age, " he said to himself, "it would sound better. He's more like Robie."

Abraham wanted to be polite and respectful, but after a long time he was too tired to keep quiet. He stood up. "I think I'd better go back to the barn and get some sleep," he said.

Mr. Malone nodded. "I was just thinking the same thing myself," he said. "We'll want to get an early start tomorrow."

Abraham left, went to the barn, and climbed up to the hayloft.

It was a clear night, and the moon was almost full. The door at the end of the hayloft was open, and the loft was full of light. He lay down and rolled himself up in his blanket, looked out at the moon and thought about the mesa.

He was going to find a fantastic jar, wrap it in tissue paper, and bring it home. He saw himself sitting at the kitchen table with Mrs. Stent and the children, ready to tell the last chapter of "The Great McGregor and the River Beneath the Mountain." Julie and Robie were drinking oat milk. He was having coffee. Jane was on his lap. He had moved the jar to the middle of the table so she couldn't knock it over. He told the rest of the story. The children loved it. He put Jane to bed and kissed her good night.

"But I won't stay there long," Abraham said, his eyes wide open. He'd sell the jar to a museum in New York or some place for a lot of money, and then he'd take another trip, maybe to Asia or Europe, and find something else.

He shut his eyes, and in less than two minutes he was asleep.

He had a dream.

In his dream he met a very old man, maybe an Indian, maybe a white man who was brown from age and the sun. They were in the bottom of a wide canyon, with steep cliffs on both sides, and the man was showing him around and giving him a lecture on Indian history. They walked into a cave, and the old man sat down. Jane was there. She took his hand and began to tell him, in a careful, quiet, intelligent way, about the man, who he was and how old. Abraham was so proud of the way she did it that he woke up smiling.

"Burros," he said as he sat up. "That's the first thing. Burros."

9

I'll tell you a story about a Christmas horse, Abraham's father said to him one Christmas Eve. It was his first Christmas in Silverton. He was eight years old.

Listen carefully, Abraham, and you can hear singing. Far away, people are singing in the chapel of a great castle. In the front pew, next to the Queen, sits the King. In the back, near the door, stands Harold, who works in the stable and is a great lover of horses. Outside it is snowing, and in the stable, eating sweet hay and listening to the music, is Jurassus, the King's favorite mare.

Everybody is singing "O Come All Ye Faithful," in honor of Christ. It sounds so beautiful that Harold wants to reach out and take ahold of somebody's hand and say, "Merry Christmas! God give you whatever you need."

The chaplain begins to read the Gospel. On a certain night long ago, he says, a baby was born in a stable, and angels sang glory to God in the highest, and on earth peace, good will toward men.

More than before, Harold wants to reach out and take hold of somebody's hand and squeeze it tight.

Everybody begins singing again. "Joy to the world, the Lord is come. Let earth receive her King." The candles make the altar look as beautiful as heaven. Harold knows that he will soon take somebody by the hand and say, "Merry Christmas! God give you whatever you need."

The chaplain blesses the congregation, and the King gets up and starts walking toward the back of the chapel. Everybody bows as the King comes by. Harold bows too, but then he reaches out and grabs the King's hand and squeezes it. "Merry Christmas!" he says. "God give you whatever you need."

The King makes an ugly face and pulls his hand away and keeps on walking.

Later, Harold speaks to Jurassus. It is late, and everyone in the castle is asleep.

"The angels sing glory to God in the highest, and on earth peace, good will toward men and horses," he says to her, "but the King won't even let me touch him. God give you whatever you need, I tell him, but he just makes an ugly face and walks away. It's stupid, stupid, stupid, stupid, stupid. God bless us, it is stupid."

Jurassus looks at Harold. "Be cautious," she says with her look. "Control yourself, please."

"How can a man be cautious with his joy in Christ?" Harold asks. "Who can put his hands in his pockets and hold back his blessings?"

Now it is early morning. Harold has saddled Jurassus, and the King has gone off into the snow for his morning ride. Christmas Day, but no matter, the King must have his morning ride.

Boom! An avalanche of snow comes down the mountain.

"Help! Help! Help!" The voice of the Queen, louder than the boom. She is leaning far out of her tower window, twisting her hands together. "Oh! Help, help, help!"

Harold. Get a shovel. Run!

Dig, dig, dig. Ah! Here is the King's coatsleeve. Reach into it. Reach deeper. Reach deeper still, and still deeper. Ah! Here is the King's hand. Grab it tight and pull. Dig some more, grab it tight, and pull again, harder. Ah!

"My dear King, you are out. God bless you!"

Dig dig dig dig some more. Now, darling Jurassus, where's your head? Here it is at last. How are you? Shake your head. I'll dig some more. We'll work together until you're free.

Can you hear them all singing again? A service of celebration in the chapel. The King's life has been saved, and the life of his favorite mare. Behind the King, in a place of honor, stands Harold, the hero of the day. Psalm XXI: "In thy strength, the King rejoices, O Lord." Joy! Thanksgiving! Music! The chaplain pronounces the blessing. Harold reaches forward with his right hand and takes ahold of the King's left hand and squeezes it. "Bless you," he says. Music! Thanksgiving! Joy!

The King pulls his hand away and goes out.

End of celebration.

Night again. Christmas night, late. Harold and Jurassus are together, saying nothing, thinking.

Through the stable door they see the King walking in the courtyard with his head down, thinking.

An idea comes to Harold, a glorious idea. He will run out into the courtyard and grab the King by both hands, and swing him around, and shout, "Merry Christmas, God give you whatever you need," and run away in the dark before the King knows what's happening.

He looks at Jurassus.

Jurassus looks at him. "I have a better idea," Jurassus says. "Get on me, and we will ride away."

"Steal you?" he says. "Steal the King's favorite horse? Ride away on the King's favorite mare?"

"Yes. Yes," Jurassus answers. "This castle is not for a man like you. It is Christmas night. God is giving you what you need the most, a horse and a long ride. Take me now, and ride away."

Harold climbs on Jurassus and rides out of the stable.

"Who goes there?" says the King.

"Harold, your majesty," Harold answers. His voice is calm. "I am taking your horse, and going away."

The King hides his hands behind his back and looks afraid.

Harold rides slowly to the castle gate and stops. "Merry Christmas," he calls back to the King. "And may God give you what you need the most." And then, at an easy pace, surprised that God should have given him such a large Christmas present, he rides away.

It was morning. Abraham and Mr. Malone and Mr. Green were having breakfast.

"The first thing to do, I guess, is to buy some burros," Abraham said.

Mr. Malone smiled. "Whatever you say, Abraham. Climbing and burros is your department."

Mr. Green, who looked a little drunk again, said nothing.

The man they went to, Mr. Sweet, first tried to sell them horses. "They're stronger than burros," he said, "and you can do twice as many things with them."

Abraham shook his head. "They're harder to feed and catch, and you have to worry about water more."

"Suit yourself, of course. I don't want to sell you something you don't want," he said, stopping in front of a stall with a big brown horse in it. "But this animal will do more for you than any two burros anywhere."

"This horse here," Mr. Green said, standing in front of

a stall on the other side of the barn. "How much is she?"

"She's my prize," Mr. Sweet said. "Three hundred and forty-five dollars. Not that I want to sell her."

"How much to ride her?"

"Two. You can see she's got no saddle on her."

"That's all right," Mr. Green said. "What's her name?"

"Red."

Mr. Green came over, gave Mr. Sweet two dollars out of a button-down pocket in his shirt, went back across the barn, and opened the stall door. He put out his right hand, rubbed it up across the horse's face and down her neck. Then, with his right arm on her neck, he led her through the barn and out into the corral.

"Excuse me," Abraham said, and followed them as far as the barn door.

Mr. Green stopped the horse in the middle of the corral and leaned his ear against her neck, as if he were listening for something inside. Then, without a sound, both his feet left the ground and he was sitting on top of her. Holding his left wrist in his right hand so it wouldn't bounce in its sling, he put his knees and feet tight against the horse's sides and began moving her in a circle. After a few times around in one direction, he turned her and set her going in the other. Then he crisscrossed the corral. He walked her slow and fast. He trotted her slow and fast. He ran her slow, and fast, and faster. Abraham never knew a horse could go at so many different speeds.

After a few minutes he took her at a slow walk to the barn door, swung his leg over her neck, dropped to the ground, and led her inside, past where Abraham and Mr. Sweet and Mr. Malone were standing.

"It's a natural gift," Mr. Malone said. "He's part Navaho."

"He fell at least once," Mr. Sweet said, "if you judge by his arm. Here, I'll show your boy some burros."

"Mr. Malone and I aren't related," Abraham said, trying to make it sound friendly and casual. "We're just working together."

"Partners, are you?" Mr. Sweet asked, and Abraham nodded.

For the next little while Abraham and Mr. Sweet, saying nothing, went from burro to burro. They all looked fairly healthy, and after carefully examining the feet and ears and mouths of six of them, and looking at their bellies for strap burns, Abraham picked two.

"Do they look all right to you, Mr. Green?" he said.

"I don't know burros," Mr. Green answered, looking down at the ground. By this time Mr. Malone had his money pouch out. The pair cost $55.

The rest of the things, tools, pans, canteens, tarps, ropes, and pack harnesses, were bought quickly, all in the same store. Abraham picked out the harnesses and the ropes, and Mr. Malone got everything else. Everything was second-hand, but it all looked good.

They carried it out on the back porch of the store,

and Abraham began packing the burros. Mr. Malone stood next to him, and Mr. Green went away—for a drink, Abraham guessed.

"What about a gun?" Mr. Malone asked after a long time.

"I don't have one," Abraham said.

"Do you think I should get one?"

"For hunting?"

"For hunting, and other things."

Abraham began to strap down the first pack. "Do you think we're going to have any time for hunting?"

"I don't know," Mr. Malone said. "Maybe we'll have to do some hunting, for some reason or other."

"We're taking eighty pounds of food," Abraham said.

"I know," Mr. Malone said. "Eighty pounds is a lot of food. And a lot of it is dried meat. Still . . ." He looked uncertain, like a baby with a spoonful of some new vegetable in his mouth. "I'll go look around," he said, and left. Abraham knew that he'd come back in a little while with a rifle, so he left room in the second pack for it.

You know, a lot of people carry guns because they don't know how to finish a sentence, Abraham's father once said to him. *If everybody knew how to put a decent sentence together, there wouldn't be such a big demand for ammunition.*

Abraham, Mr. Malone, Mr. Green, two burros, two packs of supplies, and a .30 caliber rifle crossed the

Animas River and started through Wildcat Canyon early in the afternoon. Abraham walked in front, holding the lead burro's bridle. He felt good. The animals seemed to be strong, and they were easy to handle. Mr. Malone walked beside him, and Mr. Green came behind the second burro.

On both sides of Wildcat Canyon there were mine shafts and shaft houses, but from the look of them, all the silver in the canyon had turned out to be coal. Compared to the narrow canyons around Silverton, Wildcat Canyon didn't look like a canyon at all, but like a narrow valley.

After a few miles the road began to climb. You could see farther and there was more grass, but it was rough country, full of hills and rocks and deep ravines. After a while there appeared in front of them a high, flat-topped mesa, its bare front cut across with layers of sandstone. Abraham turned back toward Mr. Green. "Is that the Mesa Verde?" he asked.

"No," Mr. Green said.

They went on in silence. Abraham began to get hungry.

"About four miles from here there's a fork where the Hesperus road begins," Mr. Malone said as the sun got lower. "There's a house there where we can spend the night."

"We could go farther than that, couldn't we?" Abraham asked. "The burros are fine. We could go ten more miles if we wanted to."

Mr. Malone shook his head. It was a hot afternoon, and the sweat on his face glittered in the sun. "Hesperus is far enough," he said.

Abraham didn't answer, but he didn't like the way Mr. Malone sounded. There was irritation and even anger in his voice, as if walking any distance was an insult to him. He sounded the way Robie sounded when he was dirty and you told him he had to take a bath.

"If I do what he says now," Abraham said to himself, "he'll be the boss. I'd rather have Mr. Green for a boss, even drunk."

He crossed to the other side of the front burro and examined his pack. Then he dropped back and looked at the second burro's pack, all the time thinking about the house at Hesperus fork and what would happen when they got there. "If I do what he says now," he said to himself again, "he'll be the boss. Let him find a soft bed if he wants to. I'll go ahead. He can catch up with me in the morning."

When they got to the house at Hesperus fork, they stopped. It was around dinnertime, or maybe a little after, but Abraham didn't care. He was going to go on. He wasn't going to sleep in a house or a barn, even if it didn't cost him anything.

"Well, here we are," Mr. Malone said, wiping his forehead, nose, and beard with a large handkerchief. "It's all right if you go on a little, Abraham, and I'll catch up with you in the morning."

Abraham was glad not to have to argue with him. "I'll wait for you by the road," he said.

Mr. Malone smiled. "Mr. Green can stay with me, just like it was last night. Where's my bag?"

Abraham went to the second burro, took Mr. Malone's carpetbag off the pack, and retied it. He said goodbye, shook hands with Mr. Malone and Mr. Green, wished them both a good night's sleep, and led the burros on down the road, happy to be alone. After a minute or so, he looked back. Mr. Malone was standing on the front porch of the house talking to someone. Mr. Green stood in the yard, waiting, with Mr. Malone's bag in his good arm.

Abraham didn't go as far as he had expected to. Now that he was alone his legs felt tired, so when he came to a good camping place he stopped. It was at a bend in the road. On the right was a high hill, mostly bare, with some grass in spots and a few spruce trees. On the left was a shallow ravine with a creek running in it, and on the other side of the ravine was a grass-covered field.

He crossed the ravine into the field, and after he had unpacked the burros he took off his shoes and socks and went down to the ravine and put his feet in the creek. The burros came down with him and drank for a little, and then they climbed out of the ravine to eat some grass and clover. In a few minutes Abraham climbed out too. With farms around, one of the burros might decide to find a barn to sleep in for the night, and he didn't want that, so he brought them close to the packs and put leather hobbles on their legs so they wouldn't be able to walk far.

He started a fire to heat some water for coffee, and while it was heating he finished the piece of bread and cheese that was left over from their lunch. When the coffee was made, he poured it in a big mug, crossed the ravine and the road, climbed to the top of the hill, and sat down facing west.

A low line of clouds ran across the horizon from the northwest to the south. The sun was down, and the last light of day was going from the sky. The moon hung directly above his head. Which part of the dark, rough horizon was the Mesa Verde? "Maybe I can't even see it from here," he said to himself. "I probably can't."

He thought of Jane and wished that she were with him so he could show her what he was seeing and tell her what little he knew about it. He'd tell her about the Spanish explorers who had crossed the Southwest, giving names to places like Mesa Verde. "You know what Mesa Verde means?" he would say to her. "It means 'Green Table.' Isn't that funny?"

She'd be fun to have around. She could ride on one of the burro packs. At night she could sleep near him, and he'd tell her stories and teach her things.

He decided to write her a long letter when he got to the mesa, telling her all about his trip there, what they saw, and how the mesa looked from the top. He'd tell her to keep the letter so that she'd have it as she was growing up. "Wouldn't it be fine," he said to himself, "if

I could travel to twenty or thirty different places, and every place I went I'd write Jane a letter. After a while she'd have a whole collection of them. She could paste them all in a book. She'd call it 'My Book of the World,' and at the same time she could write me and tell me how things were at home and what she was doing and asking me questions."

Abraham sat for a long time, until long after his coffee was cold. Then he stood up, finished his coffee, and went down the hill. When he got to the camping place, he rebuilt the fire, rolled up in his blanket next to it, put his head on a bag of sugar wrapped in oilskin, and closed his eyes. A minute later he opened them up again, thinking that maybe he ought to get up and get out the rifle and load it and keep it next to him, but he couldn't think of a good reason why, so he shut his eyes again and went to sleep.

He had a dream toward morning. In his dream he was getting ready for something having to do with Indians. He was dressed in a comfortable buckskin suit for whatever it was, but he had to have his face painted so that he could fit into the tribe. Some Indians were helping him. They kept painting his face in different ways, and painting it and painting it, but they never got it right, and after a while he woke up. It was morning.

10

Abraham sat up and looked toward the road. It was empty. Everything was quiet. Under the rim of the ravine, he knew, the creek was running, but silently. Not even the birds were making noise.

He got up, watered the burros, and packed them. He worked quickly, saving out three gingersnaps and three oatcakes from the second pack for breakfast. Then he led the burros across the creek and up onto the road, sat down, ate, and waited.

After a while Mr. Malone came along, with Mr. Green next to him, carrying his bag. Mr. Malone was already sweating, and he looked tired. It was going to be a hot day. "Good morning, Mr. Malone, Mr. Green," Abraham said. "I hope you slept well."

"I had a fine night's sleep," Mr. Malone said, "and a really good breakfast, and I'm ready for a good long hike."

They started off fast, and soon they had crossed the bridge over the La Plata River.

"From the Hesperus fork to Mancos is seventeen miles," Mr. Malone said. "There's a ranch near there that belongs to the Wetherills. You ever hear of them?"

"No, I haven't," Abraham said.

"Well, they know all about the mesa, and they're friendly with the Utes. We're getting into Ute country, you know. They were the first whites to bring anything out of it. Maybe we should go see them. What do you think? The Wetherills."

Abraham didn't like the idea. It meant slowing down, probably taking an extra day. "I don't know," he said. "Mr. Green knows where we're going to go, doesn't he?"

Mr. Malone didn't answer.

Abraham thought about Mr. Green. He imagined becoming good friends with him, finding out about him, working together with him down in the canyons, while Mr. Malone sat on the mesa top wondering what they were doing. He imagined himself saving Mr. Green's life, pulling him up over the edge of a cliff with an iron grip on his bad arm.

He looked back. Mr. Green was a few steps behind the second burro, looking at the hills to the south.

"You see something?" Mr. Malone asked.

"No."

They went on in silence for a while.

"Have you known Mr. Green for a long time?" Abraham asked.

"We're old friends," Mr. Malone said.

"He's very quiet."

"He keeps his own counsel."

"How did you meet him?"

"That's a long story, Abraham. It was an important meeting for both of us. Did I ever tell you about my first meeting with your father?"

"I don't think so."

"Well, it's time I did. I had a special place in my heart for your father. He was a remarkable man. Everybody liked him and admired him, but not everybody understood him."

He stopped for a moment and smiled. There was so much ignorance behind his smile, so much *emptiness,* that Abraham felt sorry for him.

He started talking again. He seemed to have the idea that Abraham's father was Greek. "The finest Mediterranean stock comes from Greece," he said twice, and twice he mentioned "the heritage of Athens." He called Abraham's father "a natural aristocrat," full of "courtesy," "manliness," and "strength of character." He also spoke of his "great skill in mining."

Expecting a lie, Abraham asked him when he and his father had met. Mr. Malone smiled again. "Don't you remember?" he said. "You two were playing cards, and I came in and spoiled your game. It was shortly after Mr. Stent had passed away, may he rest in peace. I stayed the evening, and after you were in bed your father and I had a long talk. I learned a lot about him that night. We really became friends. He was a remarkable man, you might even say a great man."

"Did you ever work with him?"

"No, unfortunately, but I knew a lot of miners who did, and they all said the same thing about him. It's a shame he didn't live to teach you all the things he knew."

"What sort of things?"

"All sorts of things," Mr. Malone said in an offhand way. "You were very young when he passed away, and there were many things you weren't capable of knowing. He was a great man. I know."

Abraham's face suddenly got red with anger. Mr. Malone was telling him he didn't know his father. This stranger who looked like a baby, this silly, stupid man who had never been in a silver mine, who knew nothing about burros or camping, who couldn't do anything but talk and wash dishes and persuade drunks to follow him around, this drifter who combed his beard, probably, and waxed it, probably, and came calling on widows and smiling, this fool who thought John Candle was a Greek, was telling him that he "knew" and "understood" him better than his own son did. "He has no shame at all," Abraham said to himself. "He doesn't care what he says, as long as it sounds good." He kept his mouth shut and waited until he felt calm again.

"Did you think my father was a Greek?" he said then.

"He had a Greek mind," Mr. Malone answered.

"He was from Italian Sicily," Abraham said. "His father was an engineer from England working for a sulphur-mining company. He married an Italian woman and stayed there. They died in an influenza epidemic in 1871, and my father came here. He lived in Pennsylvania, and after my mother died we came to Denver first and then Silverton. Did my father ever tell you any of his stories?"

"No, I don't think he did."

Abraham said no more. There was no more to say. If Mr. Malone didn't know any of his father's stories, then he didn't know him at all, and that's all there was to it.

They walked on in silence.

Toward afternoon, with no stop for lunch, they reached the western ridge of the Mancos Valley. There they stopped and looked down and ate two gingersnaps apiece.

"I still don't know about the Wetherills," Mr. Malone said when he finished his second gingersnap. "Maybe I really should go and see them. You could go on a mile or so past the other side of town and I'd catch up with you tomorrow. You and Mr. Green both could go."

"Do you know where they live?" Abraham asked.

"Not far from here. Everybody knows them. Why don't you two go on, and if I'm a little bit delayed you can wait for me."

A few hours later Abraham and Mr. Green were camped on a hill overlooking the road about two miles west of Mancos.

"We'll see the mesa soon," Mr. Green said.

It was getting dark. Dinner was over, the burros were hobbled, the pans were washed, and the fire was even. Abraham watched it.

"How far are we from where it starts?" he asked.

"About fifteen miles."

They were quiet for a few minutes. Abraham felt good. It was as if, after a long time without one, he had a friend. It didn't make any difference that he didn't know the man, or that he was maybe fifty and sometimes drunk. He felt as if he could trust him, for this trip anyway, and that was all he wanted. He had a good face.

"What does the mesa look like?" he asked.

"I can draw it for you," Mr. Green said.

Abraham came around to his side of the fire while Mr. Green pulled up grass and cleared an area of dirt to draw on.

The figure he drew was like a hand, with the fingers pointing south. "Here are long canyons," he said, pointing between the fingers. "All the main canyons have side canyons, so it's easy to get lost. The Mancos River runs down the east side of the mesa and across in front of it."

"Where are the caves?"

"In the canyon walls, a pretty good way down from the top."

"Is it hard to get to them?"

"The Indians did it. We have ropes if we need them."

Abraham studied the map on the ground. From where they were camped, there were two ways of getting to the caves. One was to climb across the wrist of the mesa and go south, reaching them from above. The other was to follow the river around the mesa and go up one of the canyon floors, reaching the caves from below.

"What's the best way to go?"

"Across the mesa and down. You don't want to camp in the canyons unless you have to."

Abraham looked up from the map and into the man's eyes. "Which canyons are the caves in?"

"All of them."

They fell silent. A few minutes later, without a word, they took canteens and went off in separate directions to wash their mouths out with water and get ready for sleep. Then they came back, took off their shoes, and rolled up in their blankets next to the fire.

Abraham didn't want to go to sleep.

"You didn't know my father, did you?"

"No."

"He died a year and a half ago. December 29."

Mr. Green said nothing.

"He used to tell stories he made up. Would you like to hear one?"

"Not tonight. Maybe another time."

"Sure. Good night."

"Good night."

11

They reached the mesa top two days later, in the middle of the afternoon, in a cold, heavy rain. It was the Fourth of July. Behind and below them was the Montezuma Valley. Fifteen miles ahead, at the south end of the mesa, were the canyons. The burros stank. Abraham couldn't remember animals ever smelling so bad before, and he worried that maybe he was doing something wrong, driving them too hard or making the packs too heavy.

There were piñon pine trees everywhere, but it took a long time to find two of them that were tall enough, strong enough, and close enough together, with an open space between, to hold a rope and tarp shelter. Mr. Malone wasn't any help at all. He made believe he was looking, squinting ahead through the rain every once in a while with a hopeful look on his face, but he never said anything. Mr. Green didn't help either. He just walked behind, with his eyes on the ground, waiting for Abraham to decide.

Finally Abraham found the right place, on a slight rise, and the two men began to help. Mr. Malone unpacked the second burro by himself, while Abraham and Mr. Green got up the rope and tarp shelter. In about two hours they had the tarp up, the burros tied in the lee of a large rock about fifty yards away, a pile of wood gathered, a good fire going, and coffee made. The piñon-pine fire burned hot and gave off a good smell. Abraham stood close to it to dry off his clothes.

After supper the rain stopped. "It's a good omen," Mr. Malone said. "Now all we have to do is find a rainbow." He pointed. "There it is, to the right of that juniper." Abraham looked and saw it right away, a light misty rainbow hanging beneath the dark clouds.

"Let's celebrate," Mr. Malone said. "I have exactly the thing." He went over to the second pack, which lay half taken apart near the back of the shelter, and took out a package wrapped in butcher paper and tied with a string. "Gumdrops," he said. "They're the last thing I bought before we left Durango."

Along with a rifle, Abraham thought to himself.

"They may be a little sticky."

Mr. Malone crouched down by the fire, smiled his

boyish smile, untied the string, and pulled back the paper. The gumdrops looked like jewels melted together.

"Take one," Mr. Malone said.

Abraham took hold of a red one and pulled, getting off a lump that was mostly red and green, with a long, glistening tail of green and yellow. Then Mr. Malone poked the lump at Mr. Green, who also took some. The three of them kept eating at the lump until it was gone, and then Mr. Malone threw the paper into the fire. They sat back, licking their fingers.

"Clayton Wetherill told me there was a cave in one of our canyons with a whole palace in it," Mr. Malone said. "It's really a small city, with the houses all built together, all in one big cave, but they call it Cliff Palace. His brother Richard found it." He looked at Mr. Green. "I guess you know where it is," he said.

Mr. Green said nothing, but kept looking at the fire.

"According to him," Mr. Malone went on, "everything's been taken out of it already. Do you think that's true?"

Mr. Green nodded. "If he says so."

"Excuse me," Abraham said. He got up and walked through the trees to where the burros were tied. It was chilly away from the fire, but he was glad to be walking and to be alone. The burros had a little mist rising off their backs, but they didn't smell as bad as they had before, and that made him feel better. He untied them and hobbled them, and they limped away to look for grass.

He thought about the children. Mrs. Stent was having a hard time with them, he was sure of that. Maybe he should have told her about the cave before he left. Well, it was too late, and it was too steep for her to climb up there anyway, and she'd have to leave Jane alone, so it was probably just as well she didn't know.

Mr. Malone came through the trees.

"Are the burros all right?"

Abraham nodded. "I hobbled them so they could graze a little. The grass isn't too wet."

"When you were alone with him when we were near Mancos, did he talk to you at all about where we were going?"

"Mr. Green?"

"When the two of you were together."

"He drew me a map."

"Did he show you where the caves were?"

"Not exactly."

"Abraham, let me tell you something. To be perfectly honest with you, I'm a little bit worried. He could just take us where everybody else has been already, and that's all."

"I thought he knew about caves nobody else knew about," Abraham said.

Mr. Malone was silent for a few moments. "I thought so too," he said then.

"Didn't he tell you he did?"

"Not exactly in so many words. He told me there were caves nobody knew about, but he didn't exactly come out and say he knew where they were."

"Oh."

"If he wasn't telling you about the caves," Mr. Malone asked, "what was he drawing the map for?"

"He was showing me what the mesa looked like."

"Where'd he say the caves were?"

"Everywhere."

Mr. Malone smiled, showing his teeth in the moonlight. "Oh. Well, then, I suppose we'll simply have to wait and see, won't we, and hope for the best?"

Abraham didn't answer, and Mr. Malone walked slowly away toward camp. Abraham watched him until he couldn't see him any more. "There he goes," he said quietly, "Mr. Malone, the Great Treasure-and-Wisdom Hunter of Colorado."

Once upon a time, his father told him one night, *on a farm in a valley in the mountains far away, there lived a farmer and his son, whose name was Jacob. The farmer was a great lover of wisdom, and Jacob, though he was not yet wise, had a very good mind, open and humble and quick.*

Often the farmer would watch his son measuring a furrow with his eye, or studying the clouds, or reading a book to the cows, or examining a handful of dirt, and say to himself, "It's a lucky man who has a son with such an eye for lines, such a gift for language, such curiosity, and such a love of learning."

Now it happened that a certain hermit lived in a cave high up in the mountains overlooking the valley. This hermit had a great reputation for wisdom. It was said that whoever brought a question up the mountain to him would come down wiser, no matter what the question was. None of the farmers in the valley knew which cave the hermit lived in, but they were all sure that he was waiting up there somewhere, filled from top to bottom with ancient wisdom.

The farmer decided that his son should go and see him. "Jacob," he said, "with the right training and some good luck you could grow up to be a wise man. You should go and talk to the hermit and learn some things."

"That's a good idea," Jacob said. "But first I should visit all the other farmers in the valley and find out if they have any questions for him. That way my climb will benefit everybody."

"Son," the father said, "you're a good boy. You won't get any questions, but you're a good boy."

So Jacob went to every farm in the valley and asked each farmer if he had any questions, and each farmer said the same thing: "No questions."

"No questions at all, about anything?" Jacob would ask.

"No questions about anything," each farmer said.

"But if the hermit has any good answers, tell me what they are when you get back."

Soon Jacob was home again. "You're right, Father," he said. "Nobody has any questions. Is there anything you want to know?"

"Yes," his father said. "I'd like to know why the barley crop has been so bad the past three years."

"I'll ask him about that," Jacob said.

The next morning he started off to find the cave in the mountains where the hermit lived. With him, as a gift, he took thirty pounds of wheat flour and four crocks of honey. It was a hard climb, and it took him five days to find the right cave, but he finally found it. The wise man was sitting in front, with a smile on his face.

"You're lucky you came now," he said. "I'm packing up to go to my winter cave in Brazil. One more day and you would have missed me. What have you got there?"

"Thirty pounds of wheat flour and four crocks of honey," Jacob said, laying the gifts down in front of him. The hermit brought them inside his cave and came out again.

"You got anything else for me?"

"No, I don't," the young man said.

"How about in your pockets?"

"Just a knife and a few pennies and a handkerchief," Jacob said.

The hermit put out his hand, and Jacob reached into his pocket and gave him everything he had.

"All right," said the hermit, "what do you want to know? I'm in a hurry, as you can see."

"My father and I would like to know about our barley," Jacob said. "It's been bad for three years, and this year was the worst."

The hermit nodded wisely. "The plow is not the furrow," he said, "nor the furrow the plow."

"What should we do to get a better crop?" Jacob asked immediately.

"One season is not the next, nor is the next the one," the hermit said, wiping his mouth. "Now please don't ask me anything more about food. It makes me hungry, and I don't want to eat until you go, which I'm sure will be very soon."

Jacob changed the subject. "What are the limits of knowledge?" he asked. "How much can one person know for sure?"

"The head is not the hand, nor is the hand the head," the hermit answered right away.

Jacob sat in silence for a while, thinking about this answer and trying to figure out what it meant. "How can you find out whether an answer is true or false?" he asked then.

"The bow is not the arrow, nor is the arrow the bow," the hermit replied, quick as a flash.

Jacob stood up. "I will go back down the mountain now and think about what you have told me," he said.

"The hello is not the goodbye, nor is the goodbye the

hello," the hermit said. Then he got up and went into his cave.

Jacob walked down the mountain, deep in thought, trying to puzzle out the meanings of what the hermit had told him. The more he thought, the more sure he became that the hermit hadn't taught him anything at all.

When he got back home, he told his father that the hermit was either a fool or a fraud, or both a fool and a fraud.

"Are you sure?" his father asked. "People, even smart people, sometimes make hasty judgments. Perhaps you just failed to understand what he was trying to tell you."

"No, Father," Jacob said. "The hermit told me nothing."

"Well, you live and learn," said his father. "Let's go milk the cows."

That evening, when the chores were done and the sun was down, all the neighbors came to visit and find out what useful answers the hermit had given to Jacob's questions. "Well," they said, "what did he tell you?"

"Nothing worth telling," Jacob answered.

"You mean nothing we'd be able to understand," they said.

"No, I mean nothing but foolishness," Jacob said, and then he told them everything the hermit had said.

"It must be a code," they said, "some kind of secret code. What does it mean?"

"Nothing," Jacob said. "As far as I can see, it's just foolishness."

The neighbors all shook their heads, said nothing, and left, looking angry.

After that, nobody spoke a friendly word to Jacob or his father. No one came to visit, or borrow a tool, and when Jacob went to ask for the loan of something, he was always refused. Soon he stopped asking.

Winter passed, and when planting time came, Jacob and his father talked over the barley question. "Let's not plant any this year," his father said. "Let's give the ground a rest. We'll put in clover and plow it under."

So they put in clover, and it grew fine. All their neighbors planted barley again, and when it was two inches above the ground it all turned black and died. Then everyone in the valley began to grumble, saying that Jacob and his father had planted clover because they knew from the hermit what was going to happen to the barley, and that they needed to be punished, and that it would teach them a good lesson if their barn burned down, or something.

A few nights later their barn caught fire and burned down. They saved their horses and cows, but it put them in a bad position. With no barn they wouldn't be able to get through the winter, and with no neighbors to help, it would be hard to build another barn. Nevertheless, they had to do it, so they set to work cutting timber.

As they worked, they talked about how they could win back their neighbors' affection. Finally, late one night, when they were sitting and drinking coffee in front of the fireplace, they decided what to do. The next morning Jacob went up and down the valley, inviting all the farmers to come to his house at eight o'clock that night.

At eight o'clock all the farmers were there, with guilt and anger and hatred and shame and curiosity and embarrassment on their faces. Jacob's father, standing by the fireplace, began to speak. "We invited you here," he said, "because Jacob is going up to see the hermit again tomorrow and ask him some more questions, and he wants you all to be there to hear, and find out whatever hidden or secret meanings there might be in what the hermit says."

"It's not a hard climb," Jacob added, "now that I know where his cave is."

The next morning they all arrived before dawn, ready to go. Each one carried a jug of honey for the hermit, and a sack of wheat flour. There was so much honey and flour that Jacob decided not to bring any of his own.

The climb up the mountain went quickly, and as they climbed, the farmers all began to act like schoolboys on a holiday, laughing and slapping each other on the back and telling each other jokes. When they got to the cave, everyone became very sober and serious-looking. The hermit had seen them coming and was waiting outside.

"Put the honey on my left and the flour on my right," he said, and all the farmers obeyed. Then they stepped behind Jacob and waited for him to speak.

"Good day, wise hermit," Jacob said. "I hope you are well."

The hermit nodded.

"I want to ask you again about our agriculture. Don't you think it would be a good idea if we all planted clover for another year, in the hope that whatever is hurting our barley will die in a fallow year?"

"The barley is not the clover, nor is the clover the barley," the hermit answered.

Jacob smiled and nodded. "Do you agree," he said, "that it would be a good idea for everyone to pitch in and help my father rebuild his barn, and do you think it would be good to have a big party afterwards, with cider and dancing?"

"The barn is not the party, and the party is not the barn," the hermit said. "Nor," he added, "is the sun the moon."

Again Jacob smiled and nodded. "Have you anything else to tell us?" he asked.

"I am hungry," said the hermit. He stood up, picked up two jugs of honey and a bag of flour, and went into his cave. He came out and went in and came out and went in again until he had picked up all the honey and flour, and then he stayed inside. Jacob turned around and looked at the farmers.

"Is there anyone who did not understand what the

hermit meant?" he asked. "If so, I will try to explain his words."

"We don't need any explanations," one of the farmers said. "We understood perfectly well what he meant. We're not fools, you know."

The rest of the farmers nodded, and then they all turned around and started down the mountain. After a few steps they began talking among themselves, saying what a wise man the hermit was, and how easy it was to understand his answers, once you got the trick of listening very carefully to the questions.

"Well, my friend," one of them said to Jacob's father when they were back in the valley, "how soon can we help you raise your barn?"

"We've got the wood all ready," Jacob's father answered. "How about tomorrow?"

And tomorrow it was. The barn went up, and peace returned to the valley. After a year of clover, the barley grew well again. And all the while the hermit's reputation for wisdom got stronger, as the farmers spoke to one another about his bright, penetrating eyes, his quickness at giving answers, and the way he carried all the jugs into the cave without dropping a single one.

Every once in a while, over coffee at night, Jacob's father would say, "I wonder how things are with the hermit?"

"Well," Jacob would say, "he's got a fifty-year supply of wheat and honey, so I guess he's doing all right. As for me, I've got a hundred-year supply of his wisdom, so

I think I'll leave him alone and let him eat." And he did, and they were content.

Abraham started back to camp, and as he went, he imagined Mr. Malone sitting in front of a cave, saying wise things.

"Silverton is not Durango, nor is Durango the moon."

"A gumdrop is not a pine cone, but they are both sticky."

"My beard is not a bush, nor is a bush my beard."

After each of these pieces of wisdom, Mr. Malone would smile for a few minutes.

Abraham got back to camp, put some wood on the fire, took off his shoes, and rolled up in his blanket.

He looked over at Mr. Malone, who was asleep, an unhappy look on his face. Abraham turned over and smiled. He liked the idea that maybe Mr. Green didn't know where the right caves were. Then he'd have to hunt for them, and he'd have the fun of discovery.

Part III

12

They reached the south end of the mesa late the next afternoon and set up camp on a narrow piece of land between two canyons.

Abraham saw the caves for the first time the next morning. Mr. Green woke him up with the first light. Abraham rolled out of his blanket, pulled on his shoes, and followed Mr. Green into the trees, leaving Mr. Malone sleeping. After a few minutes, Mr. Green stopped.

"I want to take you to see Cliff Palace," he said, "but we're going the wrong way. We're on the wrong side of the canyon."

For the first time Abraham saw him smile. Or at least he thought he saw him smile. Maybe he was laughing at himself for making a mistake. Maybe he was remembering some private joke that Abraham knew nothing about. And maybe Abraham was wrong, and he hadn't smiled at all. They started walking back.

It was dark under the trees, but Mr. Green moved quickly and easily, paying no attention to the ground, like a young woman on her way to church, or a banker crossing the park on Sunday morning. They turned left and came out onto a broad, bare, stone lip that hung over the end of a canyon. They crossed it and turned left again, going along the west rim of the canyon for about a mile. Then Mr. Green stopped.

"There it is," he said.

In the opposite wall of the canyon, deep under the shadow of the mesa top, was an enormous cave, sheltered on both sides by the curve of the canyon wall. Abraham stared. After a while a few corners appeared in the darkness, and then four or five black windows and a wall. Then, near the center of the cave, he saw a round tower, broken off at the top. Finally the whole city appeared, hanging silent inside the canyon wall.

He looked at it for a long time.

It was the silence of it that struck him.

The stillness, like part of another world.

"How do you get to it?" Abraham asked.

"There's a way down from above," Mr. Green said.

"Where?"

"You can't see it from here." Mr. Green was silent for

a few moments, and then he started to walk back. "I'll show you," he said.

They went along the canyon rim the way they had come, crossed the sandstone lip at the end of the canyon, and walked south along the mesa top until they were above the city. There were a lot of large stones there which looked like bricks in a wall. At one place four or five of them were loosely set against each other. Between two of them there was a place big enough for a man to get through, and a wooden ladder leading down.

Abraham got between the stones and put one foot on the top rung.

"Be careful," Mr. Green said. "If I'm not here when you come back up, wait. It's easy to get lost."

Abraham went down the ladder to a flat rock at the bottom. He looked up. Mr. Green was no longer there. The rock led him around a corner, and then there was a steep and twisting path down between enormous rocks to a ledge in the canyon wall. He walked along the ledge, turned a corner, and there was the city.

The silence of it fell on him like a fine blanket.

A low wall, broken in places, ran along the front edge of the cave. Abraham walked on top of it for twenty steps or so and then started across the city toward a group of rooms at the back of the cave. If there was anything left in the city to be picked up or dug out, it would be back there.

When he got half way, he turned around and looked

over the city and wondered how it had grown. Slowly, probably, over thirty or forty or fifty or a hundred years, with new bedrooms and workrooms and storerooms added one by one as they were needed. How many had lived here when it was finished? A hundred and fifty? Two hundred? Four hundred? No, there had never been four hundred, he was sure of that. It wasn't big enough.

He climbed on up to the back of the cave. The room he wanted to get into didn't have a doorway, only a small, high window. The next room, which was set a little lower, didn't have a doorway either, but the room after that did. Abraham went to it and climbed in. There wasn't much light, only what came in through the door. On the floor next to the entrance was a neat pile of dust and stones and sticks and bits of leather. Someone had been in the room already and searched it carefully. "I wonder what he got?" Abraham said to himself.

On the other side of the room was a low, square hole. Abraham went to it and climbed through into the next room, which was almost completely black, and passed through into the room he wanted to search. It was empty. He could see, the moment he stepped into it, that there was nothing to be taken. Nevertheless, he went carefully around the room, examining the floor and the walls.

When he had gone all the way around, he went to the window and looked out, and in that moment the city came alive for him. Suddenly he was a citizen of the place, a cliff dweller. Men and women moved here and there carrying bags of seeds, bags of flour, and jugs of water. Women scolded children for getting too close to the edge of the cliff, and men met to talk about how things were going.

In the silence of the canyon Abraham could hear the voices of the men, low and steady, discussing crops and the season and the soil and the rain, and looking up every once in a while to examine the clouds.

Behind him, Abraham began to feel the presence of someone else in the room. It was Jane, and she too was a citizen of the city, one of the children who played too close to the edge of the cliff. In his imagination he turned around and picked her up and held her on his arm and let her look out the window with him. Together, he and she made a small family, the family of Abraham and Jane, having fun watching their friends and neighbors go here and there and do things.

After a long while he put Jane down, and her presence slowly faded from the room. The voices of the people grew quiet and one by one they walked away and the city became empty again. He turned away from the window, went over to the hole in the wall, crawled through it into the next room, and went on into the room with the doorway.

He went over to the pile of dust and bits of wood and stone and leather and started sifting through it with his fingers. After a while he found something hard, with sharp edges. He picked it up and blew off the dust and wiped it with his fingers and looked at it. It was a piece of broken pottery, light brown, with nothing painted on it. He put it in his pocket and went outside.

It was bright. The sun was well up. He looked across the canyon and saw two other caves with walls and windows in them. Both caves were very small, but people had lived in them once and then gone away for some reason, leaving them empty. There were no ladders or ropes leading to either cave. That was good. It meant that no one else had been in them yet, probably.

"It can't be too hard to get down there," Abraham said to himself. "The people who lived there had to get up and down."

He looked up at the mesa top to find a landmark, so that when he went around he'd know when he was above the caves. Directly over the right-hand cave there was a dead spruce tree, higher than everything around it and completely bare. That was the place to start looking for a way down.

Abraham put his hand in his pocket, to make sure the piece of pottery was there, and then started walking across the city. When he was almost out of it, he stopped. There, against the front wall, was an empty, rusty bean can some treasure hunter had left behind. He picked it up and threw it out into the canyon. It hit the bottom with a hollow sound, like the sound of the tin bell at the Stents' front door.

• • •

Abraham had to wait a long time on the mesa top before Mr. Green and Mr. Malone came.

"Did you find anything?" Mr. Malone asked.

"Nothing much," Abraham said. He took the piece of pottery out of his pocket. "Just this."

"Did you look everywhere?"

Abraham shook his head. "Only three rooms, but I'm sure that every room has been looked in."

"What's it seem like?"

Abraham didn't know what to say. "It's big," he said, and then he looked at Mr. Green, hoping the man would say something. But he didn't. He just stood there, looking and waiting. Mr. Malone turned to him and smiled. "Where should we go from here?" he said. "Just tell us where, and we'll go."

"You want pottery?" Mr. Green asked.

Mr. Malone looked surprised and annoyed by the question. "We haven't really begun to look for it yet," he said. "Is there something else you think we should be looking for?"

"Not that I know of," Mr. Green said.

"Well, then, I guess we have our job laid out for us, don't we?" Mr. Malone said. "So, where do we begin? I suppose we just set out and look in the caves one by one." He paused. "First we have to think. The best plan, I suppose, is to start where we are. Or should we start somewhere else?"

"Maybe we ought to start on the other side of this mesa and work around," Abraham said.

"From east to west," Mr. Malone said. "That's a good idea. It has a good *sound* to it."

13

The next few days Abraham worked harder than he had ever worked in his life. He had to learn to climb with ropes. Mr. Green knew a little about it, but not much, and Mr. Malone didn't know anything at all. Things kept going wrong. Ropes got snagged, or turned out to be too short, and one rope kept oozing grease. They would work for an hour setting a rope, with Mr. Green tying knots very fast and tight with one hand, and then Abraham would go down it and find himself hanging in the air eight or ten feet away from where he wanted to go, and they'd have to set the rope again.

The second day they forgot the shovel and Abraham had to go back for it. The same afternoon he dropped a glove down into the canyon and burned his hand sliding down a rope. The next morning one of the burros went lame.

The dust in the caves was the worst thing of all. It rose around his shovel in thick clouds, drying his throat and stinging his eyes. Sometimes it was so thick that he couldn't see past his knees. Every once in a while Mr. Malone would call down from the mesa top and ask whether he had found anything. "Nothing yet," Abraham would yell back, and keep on digging.

On July 12 they moved camp, going north around the end of a long canyon and then coming south again. The next afternoon Abraham found, and broke, his first piece of pottery. He was down in a wide, low cave, like a slit in the side of the cliff, not far from the top. The cave had five rooms, four square ones and a round one with no ceiling, and he was in the biggest one.

Mr. Green had made him a box, so that he could shovel up dust and junk, carry it to the edge, and spill it down into the canyon. He was sweating, dirt was caked around his eyes, and he was short of breath. He pushed his shovel into a big pile of dust and small stones in the corner. It hit something hard and immediately went through.

He knew right away that he had broken something. The only question was how big the thing was, and how beautiful it was. He put the shovel down and started to clear out the corner with his hands. After a few minutes he could pick up what he had broken, a squat vase, with a black design around it, not big and not beautiful, in five pieces.

He put the pieces in the middle of the floor, picked up his shovel, and smashed them some more, until there were no big pieces left. Then he put them on top of the other rubble in the box, dragged it outside, and dumped it over the edge and down into the canyon.

Then he sat down outside the cave, waiting for the dust to settle and trying to think and forget how thirsty he was. He had been down in six caves, counting this one, and he hadn't found anything, except one vase, which he had just broken, worth maybe forty or fifty dollars. He saw himself spending the summer walking from cave to cave all over the mesa having strange accidents: dropping his shovel on a water jug, crushing a vase with his foot, dumping a beautiful drinking mug down into the canyon with a load of rubble, sitting on an Indian chair and smashing it to bits.

He looked at a spot at the far end of the cave, where the roof and the floor started to come together, and saw water. It was falling through the air, silently, in a steady, thin stream, out of a crack in the roof. He went over to it, put his hands under it, and washed all the dirt and dust off them. Then he washed his face three or four times, until it felt clean. Then he went and got his shirt where he had left it on a wall, and dried his hands and face, and then, finally, he put his mouth under the water and drank. It tasted wonderful.

When he was through, he stood up straight and looked

at the cave dwelling. He suddenly thought of the Great McGregor, the Lone Hero of Colorado. Here he was, alone, on the side of a mountain, in front of a cave. Abraham Candle, the Lone Pottery Smasher of Colorado. He had just finished smashing a jar worth forty dollars or more. Well, if there was one jar, there were more jars, in this canyon or the next one or the next one. He'd start to be more careful now, and he'd find them.

"Abraham?"

It was Mr. Malone calling down from the top of the mesa.

"I'm here!" he shouted back.

"Find anything?"

"I just now found a jar."

"Bring it up."

"I broke it."

"How did you do that?"

"With my shovel."

There was a pause. "You've got to be more careful, Abraham."

"I suppose you're right," Abraham yelled back. "It'd be a shame to break them all."

"Maybe I'd better come down," Mr. Malone shouted.

Abraham didn't answer. He knew Mr. Malone wouldn't come down. The man hated heights, and he also had a bad knee—hurt, he said, in a carriage accident in Philadelphia, Pennsylvania.

Abraham went back to his shovel and began working again, but much more carefully, pushing the shovel along the floor of the room and easing it under the dust and rubble. It was a much slower way to work, but it was safer and it raised less dust. In twenty minutes he found another vase, a little smaller than the first one, and a mug with a checkerboard design. He took them to the side of the cave, where the spring was running silently, and washed them. Then he had a drink out of the mug. "Good mug," he said to himself. "It doesn't leak."

By the time the sun started to go down, he had found three more jars. In the bottom of the biggest one was a hard, dry piece of corn, which he put in his pocket. As he found each jar, he took it over to the narrow string of water, washed it, and drank a swallow out of it.

"Abraham?" Mr. Malone called down.

"Here I am."

"Did you find anything?"

"Four jars and a drinking mug."

"Four?"

"Four and a drinking mug."

"A drinking mug?"

"A drinking mug."

"Wonderful."

Abraham decided to carry them up, one at a time. The way up was pretty easy. There was a wide, steep ledge that led to some stone steps cut into a crack in the canyon wall. At the top of the crack you climbed through the branches of a fallen cedar tree, and you were up.

"Four vases, forty dollars a vase, and ten or fifteen

dollars for the mug," he said to himself. "Ten. That's $170 for the three of us." He picked up a vase, unbuttoned a button on his underwear shirt and put the mug inside, and climbed up to the mesa top.

Mr. Malone was waiting for him. He smiled, and it was a good smile. There was real happiness on his face. "Good boy," he said, as if Abraham were a dog he liked a lot. "You've got three more down there? Well, we've struck it rich, I guess."

"Do you know where Mr. Green is?" Abraham asked.

"Scouting."

"What for?"

"He ought to be looking for water. When we go to the next canyon, we'll have to move camp somewhere else. Do you think there might be some more pottery down there, other than what you've already got? There could be, I suppose."

"I don't know," Abraham said. "There are two rooms I haven't looked in yet."

"What did the one you broke look like?"

"About like this one. Are we meeting Mr. Green back at camp?"

"You don't want to do any more digging today? It certainly has been our lucky day, hasn't it?"

"I'll get the other three vases," Abraham said. "I can leave the shovel down there for tomorrow." He unbuttoned his underwear shirt, took out the mug, and put it on the ground.

• • •

All the way back to camp Mr. Malone talked about the fact that they were "making progress" now. "The treasures of the mesa are just now beginning to open up," he said, lifting up the piece of pottery in his right hand. "It's just beginning, just beginning."

When he got near camp, he stopped. "I wonder. Should Mr. Green get quite as much as we do? He certainly isn't helping very much. But, no. No. We should share and share alike. That was our agreement, and a man has to live up to his agreements, don't you think?"

Abraham said nothing.

"He's a good man. Fair is fair."

"We need him," Abraham said, and started walking again. "He cooks, he sets ropes, he carries your bag around, he looks for water."

Mr. Malone walked along next to him and said nothing more.

Abraham was angry and puzzled. He was thinking of Mr. Green. He saw him in his mind carrying Mr. Malone's bag. Why did he do it, with only one good arm? Abraham didn't like it, not at all.

14

The next day Abraham brought up two large jars, and the day after that he found a stone ax and three more jars. The following afternoon, while he was working in another cave in a narrow side canyon, he fell.

He had gone down by rope early in the morning and worked until the middle of the afternoon and not found anything. Still, it was a promising cave. No one had been in it, as far as he could tell, since the Indians had gone. He was sure that if he dug long enough he'd find something good. He was walking along the edge, not watching carefully enough, and stepped off.

He fell about ten feet, hit a slope of loose rocks, rolled a long way, trying to stop himself with his arms, and then went banging into a flat boulder, twisting his left leg under him.

For a little while, nothing hurt. Then his left knee started, and his left shoulder, and his right hand, which was bleeding.

"Abraham? Abraham?" It was Mr. Malone. His voice sounded far away. Abraham had the feeling that maybe he had been calling for a long time.

"I'm here," Abraham yelled as loud as he could.

"Did you find anything?"

Abraham shook his head. "Not yet," he yelled. "Is Mr. Green there?"

There was no answer.

"Tell Mr. Green I want him," Abraham shouted as loud as he could.

He turned over and straightened out his left leg. "If it bends, it can't be broken," he said to himself. He didn't completely believe it, but it made him feel better. He sat up and suddenly felt sick and dizzy. He shut his eyes until the feeling went away, and then he opened them and looked around.

He was about half way between the mesa top and the canyon bottom. "There might be some water at the bottom I could put my leg in. I wonder where my shovel is?" He saw it, caught in the branches of a dead tree about fifty yards farther down. He decided to go that way. It would be easier, and when it came time to climb back up, he could use the shovel to lean on if he had to.

The way to the bottom was longer than he had thought, and when he got there, night was coming. That worried him. He didn't have a coat, and he had no matches to start a fire. His left knee was swollen up and throbbing with pain. He wasn't worried about dying, or even about getting very sick, but he didn't like the idea of being alone all night in a dark canyon, cold and in pain.

He got to an old spruce tree, shoveled together a pile of leaves and pine needles, and sat down on it. He was in a fairly clear spot. If Mr. Green came after him early in the morning, he'd be able to see him easily. "I wish I had some matches," he said to himself.

To take his mind off his pain, and find out as much as he could about where he was before it got dark, he began to look carefully around. About twenty yards in front of him was a clear stream with grass growing in it. About a hundred yards beyond the stream was the opposite wall of the canyon. The ground between the stream and the canyon wall was full of stones, brush, and small dead trees.

He leaned over and turned around to see what was behind the tree. There was a rough, sloping area, full of big rocks. Between two large rocks was a dark space that looked like the entrance to a cave. If he hadn't been sitting where he was, he wouldn't have seen it, and even then he couldn't be sure it really was a cave. He bit his lip, partly from pain and partly because he was thinking.

"I'll have to look at that," he said to himself. "Not now."

Then he turned his head and leaned back against the tree trunk. He felt dizzy and shut his eyes. When he opened them again, it was almost night. He was cold. His leg hurt. There was just enough light left for him to see across the canyon floor to the opposite wall. It looked impossible to climb.

When he opened his eyes again, it was night. He was still sitting up, and there was a hot fire burning next to him. Mr. Green was on the other side of the fire.

"Good evening," Abraham said.

Mr. Green nodded.

"It's night."

Mr. Green laid a piece of wood on the fire. "It's half way to morning," he said.

"I appreciate you coming."

Mr. Green looked over at him. "I saw you fall from the other side of the canyon. Do you want some coffee?"

"Yes, please."

Mr. Green poured half a mug of coffee and handed it over to him. Abraham tried to take it with his right hand, but that hurt too much, so he took it with his left. His back was sore from resting against the tree. He leaned forward away from the tree trunk and toward the fire, and sipped the bitter coffee.

"Is that what you do sometimes, watch from the other side?"

Mr. Green nodded. "When you're through with your

coffee, you can lie down and sleep through the rest of the night. I brought two blankets."

Abraham leaned back against the tree again, put the coffee mug on the ground, and shut his eyes. When he opened them again, he was wide awake. He put his hand to his face. There was a cut over his left eye that he hadn't noticed before.

It was still black night, but it felt close to morning. Except for his right hand, and his left knee, and his back, where he was leaning against the tree, nothing hurt. He leaned forward toward the fire. "Have I been asleep for a long time?"

Mr. Green looked over at him. "An hour or two. It's almost morning."

Abraham sat quiet for a little while, staring into the fire. Then he looked at Mr. Green. "I wonder if I could ask you something," he said.

"Sure."

"I know it's none of my business, but I've been wondering why you came out here."

"Money. How about you?"

"Money, I guess. Did you want it for anything special?"

"To live on. Maybe to buy a horse."

"Are you really part Navaho?"

Mr. Green shook his head. "No, but a Ute Indian brought me up. My mother was dead, and my father was away a lot, buying and selling, and the Indian ran the house."

Abraham watched the fire for a few minutes.

"What did you do when you first left home?"

"A lot of different things. I was a cowboy more than anything else. I stayed one place nine years, and another place five. Then I had a fall, and that was the end of it."

"What'd you do then?"

"Came back to Colorado. I grew up in Mancos. Last year some people hired me to bring them out here and show them the caves. I knew the mesa from when I was a boy."

"Were the caves any different then?"

"When I was a boy? I didn't even know about them then. Nobody did. They were here for hundreds of years, and nobody saw them until two years ago. Hardly anybody ever came out here."

"How did you know where they were?"

"Clayton Wetherill told me."

"Mr. Malone thought you knew all about them."

Mr. Green shook his head and smiled. Abraham didn't like to see him smile. It didn't look natural on him. "I never said that to him. I went up to Silverton and sold a jar to Finney's Store in the middle of June. That's how we met. He came and found me the next day. He wanted me to do two things, show him the caves and carry his bag. I told him I didn't know anything more about the mesa than a lot of other people knew, but he didn't want to hear that."

"Why did you say you'd carry his bag?"

"Because he asked me to, and I wasn't putting in anything. You were putting in fifty dollars, and he was putting in fifty dollars, and I wasn't putting in anything. I don't mind. I've got nothing of my own to carry."

"I don't like to see you do it," Abraham said. "I don't see why he asks you to."

"Every great leader of every great expedition has a local native to carry his bag for him," Mr. Green said, and they were quiet again.

Abraham turned his head to the left. Down in the main canyon, he could make out some light. Morning was beginning. He looked back at Mr. Green.

"Do you know how long he wants to stay here?" he asked.

"He wants a wagonload," Mr. Green said. "I guess we all do."

"Do you think he'll be able to sell it? He told me he might take it to Denver, where the prices are higher."

"He told me that, too," Mr. Green said. "Two years ago the Wetherills went to Denver to sell. Nobody'd buy until they brought in a mummy. Then with the mummy somebody bought the whole lot for three thousand dollars. It's beginning to get light. Are you hungry? I brought some oatcakes."

15

Before they started to climb up out of the canyon, Abraham looked around to see if there really was a cave back in the rocks behind him. He had to look hard. Even in the clear morning light the entrance was hard to see, but it was there. He couldn't tell how deep it was. The only way to do that would be to climb in.

They got up and got started toward the end of the canyon. That was the way Mr. Green had come down, so he was sure of it. Abraham fell a couple of times at the beginning. The second time, he opened up a cut on his right hand and they had to wait for it to stop bleeding.

"Don't handle the burros until the scab is tight on

that," Mr. Green said. "And let me carry the shovel, so you have at least one good hand free."

"How about you?"

"If I start to fall, I'll just let it go," Mr. Green said. "How's your knee feel?"

"Not so bad. Let me carry the blanket roll on my back. It won't get in my way."

They stopped around noon. They were half way up. Mr. Green still had hold of the shovel. "How's your knee?" he asked again.

"It's all right," Abraham said.

They ate two more oatcakes, drank some water, and started slowly climbing again.

It was late afternoon when they got back to camp. Mr. Malone had a fire going and some coffee on. He came over to Abraham at a fast walk. "I was worried about you," he said, with a friendly, welcoming smile. "Are you all right?"

"My knee is a little bit sore, that's all," Abraham said, sitting down on his own blanket. He was glad to see it.

"How long do you suppose it will be before it's all right again?" Mr. Malone asked.

"I don't know," Abraham said, looking at Mr. Green. "Do you think it will be all right tomorrow?"

"Probably in two or three days," Mr. Green said.

Abraham looked at Mr. Malone. "Two or three days, I guess," he said.

• • •

For the next three days Mr. Green went scouting on the west side of the canyon while Abraham stayed back at camp with Mr. Malone. He expected him to be nervous and unhappy, but he wasn't. On the contrary, he was friendlier and more at ease than he had been since leaving Silverton. He started talking again about the "hidden wisdom of these ancient people." "How wonderful it would be," he said on the second afternoon, "if their message could be shared with all the world. One could write a book, and call it *The Truth of the Vases of the Mesa Verde,* and people would read it all over the world."

The pottery stood in a row at the back of the tarp shelter, and Mr. Malone spent a lot of time there looking at it, picking jars up and turning them around and mumbling to himself.

"I'm only an amateur at languages," he said after dinner one evening. "I know a little French, some German, and a little bit of Italian, but I'm sure that the square designs have to do with order, government, and so on, and that the round designs have to do with art, and philosophy, and religion. I'm sure of it."

When he wasn't talking about pottery, he was talking about Mrs. Stent. "A remarkable woman," he said about ten times a day.

On the third day Abraham took a short walk around the camp to test his knee out. After half an hour he came back and told Mr. Malone that it was all right again.

"Where do you want to go?"

"Where I was when I fell. There ought to be some things there."

"Is it safe?" Mr. Green asked.

"That's important," Mr. Malone said. "We don't want you hurt."

"It's not dangerous," Abraham said. "I just didn't watch where I was walking before."

The next day he went back down and hit real treasure. Before noon he had dug out three large pieces of pottery in perfect condition. Late in the afternoon, in the last and smallest room, he found another large jar and two small ones. When he got them all up to the mesa top his knee hurt, but he didn't care.

That night, looking at the row of pottery in the firelight, he began to calculate how much money he was going to make. Fifteen pieces, at forty dollars apiece, made six hundred dollars, two hundred dollars apiece.

And with thirty pieces of pottery, twice that much.

The next morning, while the coffee water was boiling, Mr. Malone said he was going back to Mancos. "We're going to need more food, and different kinds of food, and maybe I can arrange for a wagon to come out in a couple of weeks. We're going to need a wagon, I can see that." He smiled a happy smile.

In an hour he was gone, taking a burro with him. Abraham worried that he might overload the animal coming back. He saw it with an enormous paper sack on its back, 120 pounds of gumdrops, and a dozen boxes of ammunition. Well, there was nothing he could do about it, so when Mr. Malone got out of sight among the trees, he put it out of his mind.

That morning he went into the last two caves on the east side of the canyon they were working. Both were small, and both had been dug in before. Just after noon, he and Mr. Green went around to the west side. "There's a large cave beyond the turn," Mr. Green said as they crossed the lip at the end of the canyon. "It's a tricky way down. I'll show you."

In a quarter of a mile they came to a crack that went twelve or fifteen feet into the mesa top. Mr. Green stooped down next to it, put his good hand on the other side, and swung down into it. He went so fast that Abraham thought, for a moment, he had fallen in.

Then Abraham put his hand across and followed him. The crack got wider as it went toward the edge. On the right-hand side, near the edge, there was a gap. Mr. Green stood there waiting for him. The gap was like a doorway. Beyond it there was a slight drop onto a long, sloping ledge. At the end of the narrowest part of the ledge was a cave. It had nine or ten rooms in it. In one of the far rooms, bent over, was a man digging with a shovel. There was a lot of dust in the air. Abraham and Mr. Green watched until the man turned around.

"Afternoon," he said. He was about twenty-five, short, and dressed like a ranch hand, with high shoes and a big brimmed hat pushed back on his head. He had dark hair and one gold tooth.

"Good afternoon," Abraham said.

The man came forward and put out his hand. "My name's Fred Nass."

"I'm pleased to meet you," Abraham said. "My name's Abraham Candle." They shook hands, and Mr. Nass's eyes flicked over to Mr. Green. "This is Mr. Green," Abraham said.

The two men shook hands.

"You here for the same thing I'm here for?"

"I guess so," Abraham said.

"This is the first time I've been up here. My boss comes up every once in a while. He's a lucky man. He always picks up something or other. They say you can sell some of the things up here for a good price. You know anything about that?"

"That's what they say," Abraham said.

"How much would a good thing, like a jar or something, get?"

"That depends on where," Abraham said. "There are different prices in different places. Are you camped up on the mesa somewhere?"

"I'm fixing up a couple of line cabins on the river. I just thought I'd take a day off and come up the canyon and climb up here and see what I could find. Is there anybody else around?"

"Not that I know of," Abraham said. "Is it pretty easy to get up here from below?"

"Pretty easy. It wasn't hard." He leaned a little closer

and spoke in a lower voice. "You know any better places to look? I can stay another day if I want to."

"All the rest of the caves on this side you have to use ropes to get down to, except one," Mr. Green said. The two men stood looking at each other for a few seconds. "We'll go some place else," Abraham said then. "Good luck."

He turned around, and Mr. Green went ahead of him along the ledge. "He won't find anything," Abraham said when they got back up to the top.

"Why not?" Mr. Green asked.

"A lot of people have already been there," Abraham said. "You can tell by looking around."

They moved along the mesa top to the second cave, and Abraham went down by rope. By the time he was through there, the canyon was in shadow right up to its rim, and it was time to quit. He went across to the third cave, which was connected to the second cave by a ledge, and left his shovel there for the morning. Then he went back and climbed out.

All through dinner he thought about Fred Nass. He didn't like doing the same thing Fred Nass was doing. It made him feel like a thief. The mesa didn't really belong to anybody, and the Indians had been gone for hundreds of years, driven out, probably, by too many years of too little rain, but still, for the first time, he felt that maybe he was taking things that ought to be left alone.

Every morning since coming onto the mesa he had seen buzzards floating on the wind currents above the canyons. He thought of himself now as a buzzard, floating over the mesa with a lot of other buzzards, picking up what he could find and carrying it away. It was getting dark, and the sky was cloudy. He thought it might rain during the night.

"Would you like to play some cards?" he said, reaching into his pocket.

"Sure," Mr. Green said. "What do you want to play?"

"Blackjack?"

Mr. Green nodded, Abraham shuffled, and they began to play. After a while they switched to gin rummy.

"You know what?" Abraham said during the second hand. "I saw you on the street the day we left on the train and I thought you were drunk."

"I was drunk," Mr. Green said. "I drink a lot."

Abraham didn't know what to say to that, so he changed the subject. "My father and I used to play cards until late every Saturday night. We'd drink coffee and play half the night."

Mr. Green studied his cards and played one. "Mr. Nass is with us," he said quietly. "Over near the burro. He was in back of the shelter twenty minutes ago, but he moved. He won't bother us. He wants us to go to sleep so he can pick up a few pieces of pottery. Just keep playing and ignore him."

"Shouldn't we do something?" Abraham asked.

"We'll play cards as long as we want to, and then when we're through, you go to sleep and I'll stay awake. That way he'll know that we know he's there, and go away. He won't hurt anybody. He just wants to make a little extra money."

"I guess he's got as much right to this pottery as we do," Abraham said. "I mean, it isn't ours, just because we found it and dug it up. We haven't got any right to it."

"Who does?"

"The Indians, I guess. And if there aren't any more Indians, then maybe the mesa owns it. This way it's just getting picked up and spread out and sold all over the place."

"If Abraham Candle doesn't dig it up," Mr. Green said, playing his final card, "Fred Nass will."

"I'm not saying I don't want to dig it up, but it's a little like being a vulture. At least it feels that way." Abraham paused. He picked up the cards and started shuffling them. "Is he still in the same place?"

"He won't move. He's found a spot he likes. Why don't you get ready to sleep? You're tired."

"I'll sit up part of the time," Abraham said.

Mr. Green shook his head. "You work all day, and I don't," he said.

"You sat up all night with me when I hurt my knee."

"I'm an old man," Mr. Green said, with a smile that looked as if it hurt him. "Old men know how to sleep sitting up."

"How old are you?"

"Forty-seven."

A thought ran through Abraham's mind. "You're responsible for your face. You're over forty, and you're responsible for your face." He looked at Mr. Green's face carefully for a few seconds. It looked to him like a mask that had been broken once and put back together again. Then he stood up, got a canteen, and went away from the fire to wash out his mouth and get ready for sleep.

After he had rolled up in his blanket, he was quiet for a few minutes. There was something he wanted to say, but he didn't quite know how to say it. "It's a pleasure to know you, Mr. Green," he said finally.

"It's a pleasure to know you, too," Mr. Green said. "Now go to sleep."

16

In his dream that night he was taking Mrs. Stent to the children, who were down in the cave at the bottom of the canyon. They kept stopping at other caves on the way, and Abraham talked to her about the Indians, telling her things he was surprised he knew. "Somewhere there's a hermit who knows all about everything," he said to her.

The dream went on, and they didn't get to the cave at the bottom of the canyon. But Mrs. Stent didn't seem to mind. She was very cheerful.

"She's all right. She's a pretty good walker," he kept saying to himself.

He was a little sorry when the dream ended and he

woke up. Not that it was so much fun climbing around with Mrs. Stent, but every once in a while during the dream Jane would come in and he'd walk a little way holding her hand and that was nice.

17

Three days later Abraham brought in ten jars, all from the last cave on the west side of the canyon.

"Tomorrow I'm going to take a day off and go for a hike," he said that night. "There's something I want to see."

"Take some food and matches," Mr. Green said.

The next morning he left early and walked east around the head of one canyon and across to the side canyon in which he had fallen. It took him an hour and a half to get down to the canyon floor, even though his knee didn't hurt much any more. Then he looked for the tree against which he had sat that night. When he found it, he climbed up to the cave entrance and went inside a few steps. It was pitch black. He couldn't tell whether the cave was short or long. "I'll have to make a fire," he said to himself. He went outside, picked up an armful of dry wood, built a small pile about five feet inside the entrance, and got it going with his first match. For a few minutes he worked to get the fire right, and then he stood aside and looked toward the back.

The cave was twenty-five or thirty feet long. It had a flat floor, and walls which were straight at the bottom and sloped in to meet each other two or three feet over his head.

The fire crackled and popped, making a hollow sound in the cool, dry cave. His shadow, thrown against the right wall, danced and jumped. He took two steps forward and then stopped. About half way back in the cave someone was sitting up against the wall. Abraham was not surprised. Hidden caves were supposed to have mummies.

He thought of money. "Five hundred dollars at least," he said to himself. He went and crouched down opposite it. It was a man, he thought. His legs were straight out in front of him, and his arms at his sides. Some small pieces of dry cloth and a woven mat in four or five pieces lay in his lap. His head was tilted to the left, as if he were thinking. There were tufts of short hair in different places on top of his head, but most of it had fallen out. There was a mean look on his face. His upper lip was pulled back from his teeth, and the skin was stretched tight across his skull, making him look like an angry, narrow-faced dog.

"I'll bet your legs would break right off if I didn't move you right," he said.

He sat looking at him until the fire burnt low, and then he got up and put more wood on it and came back and sat down in front of him again. "What were you doing here? Were you hiding from somebody? Were you sick, and you came here to die? I hope you don't mind me just coming in like this, not being an Indian. Have you been here a long time?" He stood up. "Where do you keep your food and water?"

He went slowly back farther into the cave, where the fire didn't throw much light. Way in the back, where the ceiling was so low he had to crawl, there were two big jars. He tipped one over toward the light and looked in. It was empty. Then he tipped the other one over. It was half full of corn.

He took out a handful and brought it back to the fire. His heart was beating fast. Somehow this excited him more than the mummy did. Food that you could still eat and get strength from, five hundred years after it was picked. Each kernel was dark yellow at the big end and dark brown at the narrow end. "If I had a pot," he said, "I'd pound some with a stone and boil it."

He turned around and looked back at the man. He imagined him in Finney's window with a card on his lap telling what he was. He put the idea out of his mind and looked back at the corn in his hand. "He looks just like a mean, angry dog," he said to himself, "and probably when he lived he was a fine man, and smart too. He still looks a little smart."

He stood up and began to spread the fire with his foot and stamp it out. In a minute the cave was dark again, with just a few glowing coals, like stars, on the floor, and a gray light coming in the entrance.

"I appreciate you letting me come in," he said to the old man. "Thank you."

He went out of the cave. When he got past the tree, he turned around to see if he had left any signs behind. He knew where the entrance was, but he couldn't see it from where he stood. It was well hidden. "Julie and Robie would like to have a cave like that to hide in," he said to himself. "Nobody'd ever find them."

18

When Abraham got back to camp, Mr. Malone was there, looking proud. He had gone all the way to Mancos and back by himself, leading a burro, camping out both ways, and he kept talking about it. He now knew, he said, "the lonely solitude of the trail," and "the threat of the unknown wilderness," and "the lessons a man's soul comes to in the midst of the lonely night watches."

He was as happy as he could be about the new pottery, and as he counted the jars, one to twenty-six, Abraham could see the figures multiplying in his head, and hear the gold clinking.

"There's much more in these caves," Mr. Malone said over the fire after dinner. "There are things around here worth more than anything we've gotten so far."

"Like what?" Abraham asked.

"The costume of an Indian priest, perhaps. Or a special box full of holy vessels. A leather pouch full of weapons. A mummy. In Denver two years ago Dick Wetherill sold a collection like we have, only a little bit larger, with a mummy, for almost four thousand dollars. His brother-in-law found it. Not right here, but not far away."

Abraham was silent. He could imagine what would happen if Mr. Malone saw the old man in the cave. "Well, I guess you'd better pick him up and bring him outside, hadn't you?" he'd say, smiling like a greedy baby. "I'd help you carry him, but you know my bad knee—or ankle, or whatever it is—that I hurt in Philadelphia, Pennsylvania."

Abraham tried to think. "If I was all alone," he said to himself, "how would I get the mummy up onto the mesa? Maybe I wouldn't be able to. Maybe I'd have to carry him south along the canyon floor to the river. There might be a wagon road down there. If there is, the rest of the way would be easy."

Mr. Malone went on talking, but Abraham had his mind on the mummy. "If I could take him to Denver alone by myself, and sell him myself, without anybody else, it would be all right. I'd share the money three ways, as long as I could take him and sell him myself. Maybe I can. Maybe it'll work out that way."

He looked at Mr. Malone. He was still talking. "It won't cost us too much," he was saying. "There's a Mr.

Farley who'll come up here with a wagon and bring everything into Mancos for fifteen dollars." He paused. "I told him to come in ten days, so we have our work cut out for us. Ten more days of hard, eager work." He looked at Abraham. "Is your knee all right?"

"It's fine, thank you," Abraham said.

For the next week they had no luck at all. They moved camp twice, and Abraham worked in three, and sometimes four, caves a day, but he found nothing. He thought every once in a while of his $500 mummy, but he never spoke of him. At night he thought of nothing but going to sleep.

Mr. Malone started getting nervous. Mr. Green remained quiet, calm, and detached. From sunup to sunset, Abraham did nothing but climb, and dig, and climb, and eat, and sleep, and dig some more. Over dinner he would find Mr. Malone watching him, as if he knew he was hiding something.

In the middle of the second night in their new camp, Mr. Malone shot at a skunk. The skunk shot back, making an awful stink, and lumbered away.

"This is the second night he's been around. No telling what he'd do if you didn't drive him off," Mr. Malone said, his voice trembling. He sounded like a little boy after a bad scare. Abraham was shaking too, and the sound of the gun blasts was still ringing in his ears. He pulled his shoes on, got out of his blanket, picked it up, and walked upwind. At a clear spot he laid his blanket out, sat down, and started pulling off his shoes. Mr. Green did the same in a spot nearby. Mr. Malone followed.

"Mr. Malone," Abraham said as he came near, "I wonder if you could point your gun a little more in another direction?" Without waiting for an answer, he rolled up in his blanket and turned over. But he didn't sleep right away. Before his closed eyes hung the figure of Mr. Malone, standing in the moonlight with a rifle clutched in both hands and a foolish look on his face. It was a long time before the image faded, and then he went to sleep.

When he woke up, it was day and Mr. Malone was standing over him with a sad look on his face. "The skunk got his smell on two of them," he said. "Everything else is all right. Mr. Green says there's no way of getting it off and we might as well put them back in one of the caves."

"I think so too," Abraham said.

Mr. Malone looked off toward the horizon. "That's a hundred dollars, or it could be."

"Can't be helped," Abraham said, starting to pull on his shoes.

That afternoon he carried the two stinking pieces of pottery, wrapped in canvas, down to a small cave and put them in a safe corner. Two days later, in a cave nearby, he struck another room full of treasure. It was as if the mesa, having gotten back two jars, was rewarding him with ten—three large ones, five middle-sized ones, and two small ones.

Mr. Malone was as happy as could be. "Just in time," he said as they ate dinner. "The wagon will be here tomorrow."

"I hope he can find us," Abraham said.

"He'll just work his way west until he gets here," Mr. Malone said easily. "Here's what I think we ought to do. I'll give Mr. Farley a little extra to take me all the way into Durango. It won't take me long to find a customer. You can stay here and hunt for another two weeks, and we'll meet at Mrs. Antrim's."

"You said you might go to Denver," Abraham said.

"Only if I really need to. What do you think?"

Abraham glanced at Mr. Green and then looked at the ground. He didn't want to say it was all right, and he couldn't think of a reason to say it wasn't. He was worried about being cheated. What if Mr. Malone went off to Denver and sold everything and took a train for Philadelphia? It wasn't likely, but it was possible. After all, he wasn't a young man any more. He was over forty.

"What do you think?" Mr. Malone said. "My real strength is selling, you know. That's what I'm best at. And if you stay out here, you'll have all the more chance of picking up something really good. It's only the fourth of August."

Abraham nodded and looked into the fire. "That sounds all right to me," he said, surprised that it was

August. He remembered something his father had told him once. "There's a right kind of swindler and a wrong kind of swindler," he had said. What if Mr. Malone was the wrong kind of swindler?

"I guess we'd better turn in," Mr. Malone said. "No telling when the wagon will be here. It could be early."

"I'm going to sit up a little while longer," Abraham said. He was thinking about Joseph Goodshoulder, who was a right kind of swindler, and trying to remember his story clearly.

Once upon a time there was a man, not a young man, and not an old man, named Joseph Goodshoulder. All of Joseph Goodshoulder's friends were married and had families and jobs. Joseph was not married, he had no family, and he had no job. His mother, whose name was Gerda Goodshoulder, spent most of her time knitting sweaters and blankets and rugs to sell to get money to buy food for herself and her son. Sometimes a neighbor lady would say to her, "Gerda, your boy should get married," or "Gerda, your boy should have a family of his own," or "Gerda, your boy should have a job." Sitting on her front porch, knitting, knitting, knitting, his mother would reply, "In due time, neighbor, he'll choose a wife that suits him and a job that does the same."

And sure enough, one day he did.

"My dear mother," he said to her on that day, "I have made a decision. I will marry a beautiful princess, and become a swindler."

"Joseph, you are a good boy," his mother said. "I knew that you would make a good choice in the end. I suppose, now that you have decided, you will want to start in this very morning."

"Right you are, Mother," he said. "Now that I have a destiny, I must get busy with it. First, I will go and tell the neighbors."

"Dear Joseph," his mother said, "please do me a favor and let me tell them."

"Of course, Mother," he said. "You tell them, and I shall be about my business."

A few minutes later Joseph left the house, and after a while some neighbor ladies came to call on Mrs. Goodshoulder as she sat on her porch knitting, knitting, knitting. "I just a little while ago saw your son go by," said one of them. "He was walking very fast and singing to himself. He seemed very happy."

"He is very happy," Mrs. Goodshoulder said. "You see, he has chosen a wife and a vocation. He is going to marry a beautiful princess and become a swindler."

While Mrs. Goodshoulder was telling this, Joseph was knocking on the door of a certain pig keeper, Claudius Tripe by name, who lived with his wife and daughter on the other side of town.

"I have come to ask for the hand in marriage of your beautiful daughter, the Princess Claudia," he said when Mr. Tripe opened the door.

"She's yours," said Mr. Tripe, whose mind was as quick as a meat ax. "I'll send her right out."

In a minute Claudia stood before him. Her face was washed, she had a book under one arm and a ham under the other. Joseph knelt down in front of her. "Beautiful Princess Claudia," he said, "I love you."

"Perhaps you're thinking of someone else," she said. "I am forty years old, skinny, ugly, and not a princess. Please stand up. You make me feel strange, kneeling down like that."

"Beautiful Princess Claudia," he said, "can it be that the strange feeling you feel is love?"

"It probably is," she said.

"Will you marry me?" he asked.

"Certainly," she said. "Now, won't you please get up?"

They were married on the way home, and when they got there they found Mrs. Goodshoulder on the front porch knitting, knitting, knitting, while the neighbor ladies stood around.

"Mother," Joseph said, "I have married the beautiful princess I told you about this morning, and here she is, the Princess Claudia."

"I am honored to meet you, Princess," Mrs. Goodshoulder said. "What have you got under your arms?"

"A ham, from my father, and a book of a hundred fairy tales, from my childhood. I know them all by heart, but the book has beautiful pictures, which I plan some day to show to my children."

"You, and your book, and your ham, are welcome in my home," Mrs. Goodshoulder said.

"Thank you very much," Princess Claudia replied.

"And I am very glad to meet the neighbor ladies too." She nodded toward them. In fact, she almost bowed *toward them.*

"As you can see," Joseph said, "my mother knits. I admire knitting very much."

"Then I shall learn to knit," Princess Claudia said.

"I also enjoy good cooking," he said, "and a well-made bed."

"Then I shall immediately learn how to cook, and how to make a bed, according to your taste," she said.

One of the neighbor ladies giggled. "She's no princess," the lady whispered, but very loud. "That's Claudia Tripe, the pig keeper's daughter. I went to school with her. We used to call her Skinny Tripe."

Joseph smiled. "That, no doubt, was before she became a princess," he said.

Another neighbor spoke. "Once a pig farmer, always a pig farmer—that's my way of thinking. And once a pig farmer's daughter, always a pig farmer's daughter."

Joseph started to speak, but Princess Claudia put her hand on his arm and said, "My dear friend, and good neighbor, if my husband had called me a skinny, ugly, pig farmer's daughter, I would be proud of that name, because he had given it to me. If my husband had called me a scold and a gossip, I would be proud of that name, because he had given it to me. But today, by the grace of God, my husband has called me a princess. If, by chance, I was not a princess yesterday, all good wives must agree that his word has made me one today."

"But he's a swindler," another neighbor said.

"Yes," Joseph's mother said, "he is indeed a swindler, and he wanted his neighbors to be the first to know about it."

Joseph's face suddenly clouded with sadness and pain. He went up on the porch and knelt down in front of his mother. "Mother," he said, "I must tell you something. Now that I have married the princess, I fear that I will not have time to enter upon an active career of swindling."

"Oh, oh, oh, my son," she said. "Oh, my poor, poor son. Yours was such a short career, and you could have gone far, I know."

"I know, too, Mother," he replied. "But you must understand that the princess and my marriage come before everything else."

"Of course, I understand, my boy," Mrs. Goodshoulder said. "It cannot be otherwise."

Joseph got to his feet. "All three of us will have a busy life," he said, "what with both of you knitting, knitting, knitting, and cooking, cooking, cooking. And I know the princess will want to have our neighbors visit us here at court as often as she finds it convenient."

"Indeed, dear husband, I will," Princess Claudia said, coming up onto the porch and standing beside him. "And shall we begin the court season tonight, with a ham supper in celebration of our wedding? And shall we invite all those of our neighbors who have no other engagements for the evening, and their husbands? And

shall we ask them, for the sake of beauty and elegance, to wear their wedding gowns?"

"Indeed," he said, "we shall do all those things. So now let us go and make ready."

The celebration that night was a great success. The bride and groom got a big pile of the best possible presents. The women all wore their wedding gowns, and the men looked beautiful too, and when the party was over they all went home saying that at long last some real style and elegance and nobility had come into their lives.

That night, as they lay together in bed, Princess Claudia said to her husband, "My dear love, you're not a swindler and you never were a swindler. You are a nobleman, a seeker after perfection."

"Yes, that's what I am, dear princess, a seeker after perfection. And in you I have found it."

And they lived noble lives forever after.

The fire was getting low, and Abraham poked it with a stick. Mr. Malone and Mr. Green were wrapped in their blankets, asleep. In his mind he saw the wagon coming from Mancos to take Mr. Malone and their pottery off the mesa. It made him feel lonely. Soon it would be time to go back to Durango, get his share of the money, and go somewhere else.

He imagined himself on a ship, spending his days moving around in the rigging, working with the sails, and once in a while passing the night on watch on the bridge, with a dim lantern hung by the compass. Off duty, sometimes, he'd be below decks in the crowded sailors' quarters, telling stories to entertain his shipmates as they sat smoking their pipes, listening, playing cards, and dreaming of their homes.

Did he look old enough to be taken for a sailor? Probably not.

He imagined himself on a farm in Kansas or Nebraska, nothing but wheat as far as the eye could see. He was working near the barn, cleaning the dirt off some kind of digging machine. There were children playing in the yard between the barn and the house. They weren't his children, but he watched after them and told them stories and they loved him.

He thought of Julie and Robie, and he could hardly remember their faces. But Jane he remembered. There was no trouble seeing her, and he remembered how the Stents looked together in the train station. Robie grabbing his arm to get him to finish his Great McGregor story, and Julie almost crying, and Jane really crying, screaming in fact, and Mrs. Stent telling him to come back, and on the train, thinking up a good ending for the story, which he couldn't remember now. Well, that was all right. It would come to him if he went back.

19

The last two weeks on the mesa went by very fast. Every day Abraham hunted and found nothing. He wasn't really sorry. He had already gotten a lot out of the mesa. Taking more would be worse than robbery, it would be greedy.

The night before they left they stayed up late coiling ropes, cleaning and stretching pack straps, taking down the tarp, and repacking everything. When they were through, they sat down next to each other by the fire and drank coffee.

"I saw something I haven't told you about yet," Abraham said after a while. "I found a mummy in one of the caves."

Mr. Green was silent.

"I didn't want Mr. Malone to know about it."

"I won't tell him."

"We couldn't bring it into Durango on the burros," he said. "It would get shaken up too much. We'd need a wagon. I'll show you where it is tomorrow."

"I don't want to know," Mr. Green said. His voice was calm and easy.

"I just thought maybe I ought to tell you," Abraham said.

Mr. Green shook his head and said nothing. Abraham stared into the fire. A skunk scratched around just beyond the firelight.

"My father used to tell stories. I've told you that, I guess. I still remember a lot of them. They weren't like other stories."

"How do you mean?"

"They had heroes, but they didn't do anything great or important. Some of them you might even laugh at."

"Tell me about one I'd laugh at," Mr. Green said.

"Well, he had a story about a man named Crouch, who thought the world was too small."

Mr. Green listened.

Once upon a time, many years ago, there was a man named Crouch, who thought the world he lived in was too small. "This world is too small for me," he would often say to himself. "The sky and the sun and the earth are too close. They give me feelings I don't like."

One day Crouch went to his best friend and said, "My

friend, the world is too small here. Let us go somewhere else, where it is bigger." His friend looked up at the sky, and down at the earth. "The world is the same size everywhere," he said. Crouch shook his head. "It's not the same size here," he said. "It's smaller."

"I think you're wrong," his friend said sadly. The two men stood in silence for a while. Crouch felt awful. His friend, he decided, had a small soul. "Well," he said finally, "you can do what you want, but I'm going to go east."

"East?" his friend said. "There's nothing in the east but the desert."

"The desert doesn't worry me," Crouch said. "I've got a big soul."

The next morning he got up, got dressed, and started walking east. When he got to the edge of the desert, his friend was there waiting for him. Crouch was pleased. "My friend may have a small soul," he said to himself, "but he's as faithful as a dog, and I love him."

They walked into the desert, and walked and walked and walked, until the sun was high. Crouch became very hot. He took off his shirt and threw it away. His friend picked it up. "I don't think you should throw your shirt away," he said. "You might need it."

"I don't need a shirt," Crouch replied. "I've got a big soul." And to prove it, he took off his pants and his shoes, too. His whole body was running with sweat. "As the sun gets hotter, the world gets bigger," he said. "It's a scientific fact."

He started walking again. After a few steps he took off his socks and his underwear. Then, all of a sudden, he started jumping and dancing and running around in circles. "That's it! That's it! That's it!" he shouted. "That's it! That's it! That's it!" Then he fell down in a faint. His friend knelt down beside him and put his clothes back on him and carried him home, where he washed him all over with cool water, put oil on his sunburn, and put him to bed.

The next morning, when he woke up, Crouch felt wonderful, even with his sunburn. He got out of bed, went to the window, and looked up at the sky. It was just the right height. Then he looked down at the ground. It was just the right distance away. His friend came into the room with a cup of coffee.

Crouch smiled a grateful smile. "My dear friend," he said, "I was wrong. It wasn't the world that was too small, it was my underwear." His friend handed him the coffee. "It's an easy mistake to make," he said. "An easy mistake."

"And that's the end of the story."

Mr. Green smiled. "I never knew your father," he said. "Do you look like him?"

"People used to say I had his face. He was a good, smart man."

The fire was starting to burn low. The night was cold. Mr. Green added wood, and they both got ready to sleep.

"There's a big jar of dry corn with him," Abraham said, when he was in his blanket.

"With who?"

"With the mummy."

"Oh."

"It looks as if you could eat it, old as it is. I'd like to go there again tomorrow. It's on our way. Is that all right with you?"

"Sure."

"Maybe I can bring the jar up. I don't think it's too heavy."

It was quiet for a minute. "Did you check the hobbles on the burros?" Mr. Green asked.

Abraham rolled out of his blanket before he answered. "No," he said. "I'll do it."

He was down at the entrance to the cave long before noon. The canyon floor looked almost as familiar as the Stents' back yard. He picked up some wood and went inside, set it out for a fire, and lit a match. He was in a hurry. He didn't want to keep Mr. Green waiting.

Once the fire was going, he realized that he was not going to take the jar of corn out. He would leave the cave empty-handed. This was an old man's house, and you didn't go into an old man's house and take his food, even if the old man was dead.

He walked over to him and crouched down and looked in his face. His skin was very brown, darker than the floor and as dark as the walls. "Outside of this cave, you'd look terrible," Abraham said quietly. He imagined him again in Finney's window, with a sign on his lap. "Your face wouldn't look like a face any more. Here you look like a man who looks like a dog, but there you'd look like a joke made by somebody crazy."

He went to the back of the cave, reached in the corn jar, took out one more kernel of corn, said goodbye to the old man, and left.

20

They got to Durango in three days and went straight to Mrs. Antrim's house. Mr. Malone wasn't there, but he had left a letter.

> Dear Friends,
>
> I'm back from Denver!
>
> Disregard my first letter. I plan to meet you in Silverton. It's been a fine adventure, hasn't it? I look forward to your report with happy anticipation.
>
> Cordially,
>
> Thornton Malone

Abraham and Mr. Green read it standing together on Mrs. Antrim's porch. "Was there another letter, Mrs. Antrim?" Abraham asked.

"That's the last one," she said.

Abraham nodded. "Thank you very much, Mrs. Antrim. I hope we haven't inconvenienced you."

She looked puzzled, as if she didn't know whether he was making fun of her or just being polite. After a hard look at his face, she decided he was being polite. "You're welcome," she said, and shut the door.

They went to the store where they had bought their supplies, and sold everything back for eleven dollars. As they were leaving, the storekeeper offered to buy the burros for thirty dollars apiece. "You won't get a better price anywhere else," he said.

"I guess we'll look around a little bit anyway," Abraham said, and walked on.

It turned out that the man was right. Mr. Sweet first offered them twenty-five and then went up to thirty at the last minute.

"Pick up anything out at the mesa?" he asked as he gave Abraham the money.

"A few things," Abraham said.

"Got a place to sell them?"

"I don't know," Abraham said. "Someone else is selling them for us."

"Here?"

"We talked about Denver, maybe."

Mr. Sweet shrugged.

"Don't you think he'd be able to sell anything in Denver?" Abraham asked.

Mr. Sweet shrugged again. "Denver's getting to be a big city," he said. "A lot of things going on there."

He said no more, and they went straight to the railroad station to get a train for Silverton. There was no train until the next morning, so they bought their tickets, had some soup and rolls, and then walked back along the Mancos road and camped out.

The next morning they broke camp early, hurried into Durango, ate breakfast at the railroad station, and took the train back up through the mountain passes to Silverton. When they arrived, they went straight to Mrs. Stent's and found that she was now Mrs. Malone.

"We've been married three days," Mr. Malone said, standing in the middle of the kitchen, with a big grin on his baby face. His beard was trimmed, and he was wearing a clean shirt and tie. The kitchen smelled of bread being baked.

"Congratulations," Abraham said.

Mr. Green took a short step forward. "Very best wishes, Mrs. Malone," he said. He put out his hand. "Congratulations, Mr. Malone."

Mr. Malone didn't see his hand right away, and he let it drop.

"May we give you something to eat, Abraham? Mr. Green?" Mr. Malone said. "Abraham knows how good a cook my wife is."

"How's Jane?" Abraham asked.

"Fine," Mr. Malone said. "She's spending a few days

at Mrs. Lewison's house while we get settled down here."

"She asked for you every day," Mrs. Stent, now Mrs. Malone, said.

Abraham looked at Mr. Malone. "I got sixty dollars for the burros and eleven dollars for everything else. How much did you make in Denver?" Abraham was surprised at himself for having asked the question so directly and so soon. Mr. Malone looked surprised, too.

"We did pretty well," he said, nodding. "Remarkably well, in fact, taking everything in the situation into consideration. I found someone for the whole lot almost immediately. An agent for one of the best commercial centers in Boston, so I was really lucky in that way."

"How much did you get?"

"Less per item than we expected."

"How much?"

"Five dollars. It's not an easy market, and people don't realize the value of these things. Not the general run."

Abraham was shocked. He tried not to show it. He did the arithmetic. Thirty-six jars, $5 apiece, $180. To this, add the $71 he had brought back from Durango, which made $251. If he got back the $50 he had put in at the beginning, and Mr. Malone got back the $50 he had put in, there would be $151 left for the three of them. This didn't include wagon and railroad costs. He decided to ignore them.

"Fifty dollars and thirty-three cents apiece, and a penny for Jane," he said.

Mr. Malone smiled. "Is that what it comes out to?"

Abraham put his hand in his pocket, took out his money, and spread it on the table. He picked up ten half eagles and gave them to Mr. Green. "We still owe you thirty-three cents," he said. "The bread's burning." He went to the stove, got the pan hook off the wall, opened the oven door, and hooked out three loaves. Then he took the money off the table and put it back in his pocket.

Mr. Malone smiled at him. "You and I can work out our finances later, after a good dinner."

Abraham didn't look at him. "I think I'll go see Jane," he said to Mrs. Stent-Malone. "Where are Julie and Robie?"

"Being silly, as usual," she said.

"We need to talk about them after dinner," Mr. Malone said. "We're a little worried about them."

"You come back in plenty of time for supper, won't you?" Mrs. Malone said. "Oh, Abraham, we've missed you so much. You'll never believe how much all of us have missed you."

"If you had come home first, you would have been the bridegroom," Mr. Malone said. He was not smiling.

Abraham and Mr. Green walked down the street together toward Mrs. Lewison's house. When they got there, they stopped.

"I'm going to take the afternoon train back to Durango," Mr. Green said. "No reason to stay here."

"Maybe I should go with you," Abraham said. He looked around. After so long in the light brown canyons, the gray mountains of Silverton looked strange. They made him feel homesick for the mesa. That was good. He didn't want to feel at home in Silverton. He thought of Jane, and Julie and Robie. "I guess I'll stay here for a few days anyway," he said.

They shook hands.

"I'm sorry you're going," Abraham said. "Couldn't you stay here for a while?"

Mr. Green shook his head. "I know Durango," he said. "I have nothing to do up here. Good luck."

"Good luck," Abraham said. "I hope we see each other again."

Mr. Green turned and walked off down the street, and Abraham went around to the back of Mrs. Lewison's house. Jane was there, digging in the dirt with a spoon. She had changed a lot. She was bigger and more independent-looking.

"Jane?" he said.

She looked up and started running toward him at the same time. He picked her up and hugged her. It felt wonderful. "Let's play cards," she shouted in his ear.

Abraham put her down. "I don't have any cards with me."

"Now!"

"No," Abraham said. "Not now. Later. Now we can dig up treasures and build things."

They sat down and dug together. After a while Mrs. Lewison came out her back door to hang up some wash. "Well, Abraham! I believe you've grown two inches at least."

"Good afternoon, Mrs. Lewison."

"I'll bet Jane was glad to see you. Will you be taking her home now?"

"I don't know what Mrs. Malone has in mind, Mrs. Lewison."

"Well, I said I'd keep her for two or three days, and it's three days now. It's not that she's any trouble, and I enjoy her company, but I can't keep her forever, you know."

"I'll bring her home with me for dinner."

"It's not that I begrudge her a bite of food, and she's not a hard child to govern, but it's been three days." She started hanging her clothes on the line.

Abraham looked at Jane. "We're going to go hunt for Julie and Robie."

"I don't want to."

"Come on, I'll carry you on my shoulders." He swung her up. "It was very good to see you again, Mrs. Lewison."

"Always glad to see you, Abraham."

He went across her back yard and started to climb the hill toward Julie and Robie's cave at the foot of

Anvil Mountain. When he got to the place where the hill leveled off, he stopped and called. There was no answer. He put Jane down and called again. Still no answer. He took Jane's hand and walked into the trees.

"Julie! Robie!" he shouted.

"Come and find us. Can you hear me?" It was Julie.

"I can hear you," Abraham called. He put Jane on his shoulders again and walked quickly to the cave. "Come on out. I've found you."

They came out, Julie first. They were dirty and miserable-looking, and their clothes smelled of fire. Abraham put Jane down and looked into the cave. There was a small drywood campfire burning deep inside.

"I'm not going home," Robie said.

"We've already been here two days, and they haven't found us yet," Julie said. "You wouldn't have found us either, if I hadn't called. We've got honey, bread, blankets, and everything we need."

"There's going to be a good dinner tonight and afterwards I'll finish the story I started before I left," Abraham said.

Robie shut one eye and looked up at him. "What was it about? I can't remember."

"I'll tell you after dinner," Abraham said.

"Are you staying?" Julie asked. "If you don't stay, I won't come home. My mother's married, you know."

"Come home," Abraham said, picking up Jane.

"You going to stay?" Robie asked.

"I won't tell you. Get your things, and I'll meet you at the rock."

"You've got a scar on your face," Robie said.

"I fell down," Abraham said. "Now hurry up."

"Can't you help us carry the blankets?" Julie asked.

"You carried them up here," he answered. "You carry them down."

After dinner, Abraham made both children take baths. Then, with oat milk on the table, and Mrs. Malone next to the stove, and Jane on his lap, and the children in chairs, Abraham got ready to finish "The Great McGregor and the River Beneath the Mountain." Mr. Malone, as suited the man of the family, was in the front room reading a ten-day-old Denver newspaper.

Abraham didn't really want to finish the story. The Great McGregor, with his fantastic brain and superhuman body, didn't interest him any more. But he had promised, so he began. Again, his hero went up the mountain in search of water. Again, the woman appeared, the evil Octopus in disguise. But the Great McGregor, wise as ever, saw through the disguise and tied her up and carried her back to the cave just in time to swim the underground river and save Elizabeth and Freemont. The end.

As he told the story, he got interested again, and when he got to the end he was really enjoying it. But the one who enjoyed it the most was the new Mrs. Malone. Her face, as she stood by the stove, was like the face of a small girl listening to her father. And when Abraham was through, she came over to him and kissed him on the cheek, getting hair in his eyes. "We're all so glad you're home again, Abraham," she said. "Now, children, say good night to Abraham and your new father and go to bed."

Late that night Abraham stood in the back yard watching the moon and thinking. He was free to go if he wanted to. He hadn't promised to stay. And he could get along by himself outside of Silverton. He had learned that. And what did he have here? A small room, for which he paid rent, a sloppy woman who couldn't cook, a man who looked like a baby and acted like a child, two children he didn't really like very much, and a baby who was growing fast.

Jane started to cry. Abraham went inside, into the front room, and picked her up out of her bed. He tried to get her to rest her head on his shoulder, but she wouldn't do it. She kicked around and kept crying, still half asleep. "Did you have a bad dream?" he asked. "Come on, I'll take you into my room."

He carried her into the kitchen, managed to light a lantern with one hand, and went on into his bedroom. She was dry, so he put her on his bed and pulled the blankets over her. In the light, she began to stop crying, but she still looked afraid. Seeing her, he knew that he was not going to leave. Not for a while, anyway.

"I think I'll teach you how to play blackjack before I go again. Then you'll be ready to face the world."

He sat down on the bed.

"Tell me a story," she said.

"All right, I'll tell you a story about a carpenter and a town that had bad walls and good doors."

She didn't look afraid any more.

Once upon a time, Abraham said, *a very good carpenter, carrying a sharp saw and other tools, came down the hill into the town of Fulda far away. There he built a small house, and outside the house he hung a sign saying* CARPENTER. *Then he went around looking for work. He found a lot that needed to be done. All the houses and all the stores and all the public buildings in Fulda had well-made doorways, some of which were beautiful, but all the houses and all the stores and all the public buildings in Fulda also had badly made walls and roofs, many of which were rotten.*

The very good carpenter told the people of Fulda about their walls and roofs again and again, but the people of Fulda didn't care a fig. Every time he talked to them they would say, "Yes, yes, very good carpenter, we understand what you say about our walls and roofs, but, but, very good carpenter, look at our doorways, look at our doorways!"

After a long time of telling the people of Fulda about their rotten walls and doors, the very good carpenter became discouraged and unhappy. The people of Fulda became discouraged and unhappy, too. In fact, everybody and everything in Fulda became discouraged and unhappy except the well-made and beautiful doorways, which became prouder and prouder of themselves all the time.

Then one day someone in Fulda got an idea that all the Fuldaeans thought was wonderful. They would ask the very good carpenter to start a carpenters' school. That way, some of the idle young men in Fulda would learn a trade, and the very good carpenter would not have time to tell them about their rotten walls and roofs.

The very good carpenter liked the idea. "It sounds good to me," he said, looking over his tools and his bright, sharp saw. So he gathered some students and started teaching. Soon he was so busy teaching that he stopped being discouraged and unhappy. Now he hardly ever had time to talk to the people of Fulda about their rotten walls and roofs, and so they became happy again, too. Happiest of all were the very good carpenter's students, who, under his excellent teaching, whistled and sang at their workbenches all day long. In fact, everybody and everything in Fulda became happier, except the well-made and beautiful doorways, which became unhappy and angry because the people of Fulda no longer needed to praise them.

Jane turned over and shut her eyes. Abraham kept on with the story.

One night, when everyone in Fulda was asleep except the very good carpenter, who was laying out his tools and sharpening his saw for the next day's lesson, the word went from one angry doorway to the next: "Shake!" And all over Fulda the doorways dug their toes into the ground and started shaking.

They shook, and they shook, and they shook, harder and harder, until all the people of Fulda had run up the hill shouting "Help! Help!" and all the walls and all the roofs of all the houses and all the stores and all the public buildings in Fulda had fallen to the ground. Except, *of course, for the strong walls and roof of the very good carpenter's house. His doorway, knowing the strength of the roof and walls to which it was nailed, had not joined in the general shaking.*

When Fulda was quiet again, the very good carpenter went to the town-hall doorway, climbed up to the top of it, and looked around. Fulda was a sorry sight, with nothing but doorways and one house standing under the moonlight. "Crazy doorways!" the very good carpenter said. "You could have killed somebody. Maybe you did kill somebody. So now it is time for you to be brought low, and brought low you shall be."

Immediately the town-hall doorway began to shake violently. It shook and it shook and it shook, trying to shake him down, but he hung on, and when it got tired and stopped shaking he was still on top. He climbed down, went home, and got his sharp saw. When he re-

turned, his saw shining brightly in the moonlight, the town-hall doorway began to tremble for fear. It trembled and it trembled and it trembled, and then, with much groaning and creaking, it began to bend toward him. Then, suddenly, all the air of Fulda was filled with groaning and creaking, as all the other doorways in town began to bend toward him too, until finally every doorway was flat on the ground, worshipping the very good carpenter and his bright, sharp saw.

The very good carpenter walked around the town, making sure that every doorway was flat, and then he said, "You may rise," and with much creaking and groaning they rose again.

Soon the sun came up, and the people of Fulda began to come back down the hill. The very good carpenter went here and there among them, telling them not to be unhappy and discouraged, because his carpenters could raise Fulda again, better than it was before. Then, handing his tools to his students, he said, "Go, students, and rebuild Fulda." Then he went home and went to bed.

He woke up late in the day to find his students standing around his bed with their tools in their hands. "It is done," they shouted. "Fulda is rebuilt!" The very good carpenter was amazed. He jumped up and ran outside and looked around. All the old walls and all the old roofs had been put back up again. The same nails had been used in the same nail holes. "You were right, very good carpenter," said the people of Fulda to him as they walked up and down the streets, smiling. "Your students are wonderful, and so fast, so fast!"

The very good carpenter looked at the people and said, "Excuse me, I'm leaving." Then he went back into his house, collected his tools from his students, put them all in a box, and started up the hill. When the people saw that he meant what he said, they ran after him and begged him to stay. "We need you, very good carpenter. Really we do," they said. "You have all the tools, and besides, as you have told us many times, our roofs and our walls are rotten, and getting rottener, and when they finally fall, what will we do without you to do something?"

The very good carpenter looked at them carefully for a long time. "Fuldaeans," he said, finally, "you are all very stupid. You know what a good carpenter I am, and how rotten your walls and your roofs are, but you still do nothing. There is only just so much stupidity a good carpenter can stand, and then it becomes too much. Goodbye."

With that, he walked on up the hill, and the people of Fulda returned to their houses, hoping for the best and saying to each other, "After all, our walls and roofs aren't completely *rotten, and, you have to admit, we have beautiful doorways, even if they do shake a little once in a while. So let's live as best we can."*

Meanwhile, the very good carpenter had reached the top of the hill and was looking down on the doorways, walls, and roofs of Fulda far away. He began thinking about what would happen if the doorways decided to shake again. Roofs and walls would fall, he knew, on many stupid Fuldaean heads. "I don't want that to happen," he said to himself, so he turned around and went back to Fulda, where he was welcomed with friendly smiles.

And, to this day, he still lives there. Every once in a while, the stupidity of the Fuldaeans almost makes him decide to go, but he stays, because the doorways, at least, know his power, and remember what his sharp saw looks like in the bright moonlight, and do not dare to shake.

Jane was asleep. He picked her up carefully, carried her back to her bed, laid her down, and kissed her on the cheek. Then he went back to his room and got ready for bed. Before he blew out the lantern, he looked at his face in the mirror. He hadn't seen it since June. Was it different? There was a scar over his left eye. Good. Otherwise, his face was pretty much the same. A little older, maybe. A little more finished.

He blew out the lantern, got into bed, and pulled up the blankets. The image of his own face hung before his eyes. A good face? An interesting face? A face worth telling a story about?

Yes, a face worth telling a story about.

"Once upon a time, there was a man named Abraham, who lived in Colorado. He wasn't as good as the carpenter of Fulda, but then, he wasn't as stupid as Crouch, with his underwear, either. He wanted to do something so that he'd become older and wiser and better. Besides, he didn't like it at home. So he went with some people and dug for treasure and fell into a canyon and met a mummy and made $50.33. And when he got back home, things were as bad as they had been when he left, or worse. But he decided to stay, anyway, and teach a little girl how to play blackjack, because anybody who can play blackjack can face the world. And after he had decided this, he looked in the mirror and found that his face looked a little older and better than it had before. So he blew out the lantern and got into bed and said to himself, 'Abraham, I think your face looks better because you decided to stay around and teach that little girl how to play blackjack, and not because you went away.' And that's the end of the story."

He put his hands behind his head and smiled.

It was his father's kind of story. No big heroes, no big battles, no great victories. Just a lot of work, and a somewhat better face.

Good enough. He was satisfied.